SWEEP WITH ME

Sweep with Me
Copyright © 2020 by Ilona Andrews
Ebook ISBN: 9781641971362
CS Print ISBN: 9781660140022
IS Print ISBN: 9781641971379

NYLA Publishing
121 W. 27th St, Suite 1201, NY 10001, New York.
http://www.nyliterary.com

SWEEP WITH ME

ILONA ANDREWS

[1]

Some moments in life you remember forever.

One time, when I was five, my parents told me that we were going on a trip. I looked out of the window, at the grey November sky smothered with clouds, and decided that I wasn't going. My dad brought me a pair of aviator shades, then he took my right hand and my mom took my left, and together we walked down a long hallway deep into our inn. At the end of the hallway, an ordinary door waited. We reached it, it swung open, and summer exhaled heat in my face. I shut my eyes against the bright light, and when I opened them, we stood in an alley paved with stone. Tall terraced buildings rose on both sides of us, and straight ahead, where the alley ran into a street, a current of creatures in every color and shape possible surged past merchant stalls, while a shattered planet looked at them from a purple sky.

Then there was the time when I first arrived at my own inn. It was early spring. The trees stood mostly bare except for the evergreen Texas oaks that only dropped their leaves when they felt like it. I had driven slowly, looking for the right address, and when the old Victorian came into view, I almost drifted off the road. Big, ornate and nonsensical the way Victorians often are, the building jutted against the morning sky, a dark ruin left to rot. Shingles had fallen off the roof and siding peeled from the walls in chunks. Brown weeds choked the grounds. I'd known it would be bad, since the inn had lain dormant for decades, but I hadn't thought it would be that bad.

I pulled into the driveway, got out, and began circling the house, looking for any signs of life, reaching out with my magic, but finding nothing. I was losing hope with every step. And then I rounded the corner. There, bright against the backdrop of oaks and pecans, twelve apple trees bloomed, branches heavy with blossoms. It was the moment I realized Gertrude Hunt still lived.

Today was such a moment. It didn't have the vivid colors of Baha-char or the fragile beauty of the apple trees, but I would never forget it. Sean Evans stood in our bedroom wearing an innkeeper's robe.

"Mirror," I murmured.

Gertrude Hunt shifted its magic in response. The wall in front of us liquefied, snapping into a mirror. We stood side by side, he in the copper-colored robe I had sewn for him and me in the blue robe my mother made me.

Sean was taller than me by a head. The robe covered him from his neck to his toes, but he'd left the hood down. He was very handsome, my Sean. He'd spent a long time trying to win a hopeless war. It left scars that even his body with its accelerated regeneration couldn't heal, and the shadows of its memories still flickered in his amber eyes. But when he was alone with me, like now, his eyes turned warm and inviting, his posture lost the coiled readiness, and he relaxed the way a man would in the safety of his own home.

I studied our reflection. Innkeeper robes came in a variety of styles, but these simple ones were our daily uniform. We looked like a couple. My parents had worn robes just like this, except my father preferred grey and blue.

I'd never thought I would have this. When I was younger, I had imagined myself as an innkeeper of a successful inn, but in my dreams, there was never anyone standing next to me. My parents were still missing, my sister left to marry a vampire Marshal on a faraway planet and took my little niece with her, my brother still wandered the galaxy, but I had Sean. He loved me and I loved him. We were no longer alone.

The blond innkeeper woman in the mirror smiled back at me. She looked happy.

"I like it," Sean said.

Three days ago, he'd refused to wear a robe, but I had made this one myself and now he liked it.

"You don't have to pretend," I told him.

"I like it. It's soft."

"I tumbled it with rocks for twenty-four hours. And I tattered the hem."

Sean hiked up the robe and looked at the worn hem.

Our profession was old. By chance, Earth sat on the crossroads of warp points and dimensional gateways, a convenient waypoint on the way elsewhere. We were the Atlanta airport of the galaxy. Because of this special location, an ancient pact had been made between humans and the rest of the galactic civilizations. Earth was designated as neutral ground. Nobody could conquer us. Nobody would ever enslave or devour us. The human race would be allowed to develop naturally, ignorant of any alien intelligence in the great beyond.

In exchange, Earth provided the alien visitors with safe havens; specialized hotels, each manned by an innkeeper like me, existing in magic symbiosis with our inns. Within the inns, we could bend physics and open gateways to worlds hundreds of light-years away. Outside of the inns, we were only slightly more powerful than normal people. The innkeepers had only two primary goals: to see to their guests' every need and to keep their existence secret from the rest of the planet.

Gertrude Hunt, my inn, accepted Sean because it sensed that he loved me. When he spoke to the inn, it obeyed, and it tried to make him comfortable without being asked. Sometime in the last couple of weeks, between fighting off a clan of alien assassins and nursing me back to health after the death of a seedling inn turned me catatonic, Sean had become an innkeeper. He had been an innkeeper for less than two weeks, I had been an innkeeper for a couple of years, and in that short time we had both skirted dangerously close to crossing the primary laws that governed the inns. Now the innkeeper Assembly, a gathering of prominent innkeepers, decided they wanted a closer look at me and Sean. Refusing the invitation wasn't an option.

"In the eyes of the Assembly, I've only been an innkeeper for the blink of an eye, and you even less," I said. "I don't want to show up there in brand new robes."

Sean reached over and caught me in a hug. "It will be fine," he murmured into my ear.

For a long moment I just stood wrapped in him.

"What's the worst that can happen?" he asked.

"They'll downgrade Gertrude Hunt to half a star, and nobody will ever stay with us again. Without the magic of the guests, the inn will wither."

"We'd still have Caldenia," he said.

That was true. Once a galactic tyrant, her Grace had chosen Gertrude Hunt as her permanent residence. She paid a hefty sum for it, but it didn't come anywhere near the size of the various bounties on her head.

"And Orro."

"Orro is staff, not a guest."

"And your sister and the thick-headed vampire."

That was true, too. Maud and Arland loved each other. No matter what happened I was sure they would end up together, and House Krahr, Arland's clan, would always stay at Gertrude Hunt.

"And the Otrokars." Sean kissed me. "And the Merchants."

I kissed him back.

Something banged below us in the kitchen, followed by a deep roar. "Fire!"

Gertrude Hunt must've been concerned enough to channel the sound to us.

Sean groaned. "He has to stop doing that."

"I'll go check on him."

"Wait…"

I sank through the floor, slipping through his arms, and landed in the kitchen. Sliding through walls required practice. Sean would take it as a challenge.

The delicious aroma of broth and cooking meat enveloped me. At the stove, Orro poked something in a large pot with an even larger fork. Seven feet tall and bristling with foot-long brown spikes, the Quillonian chef looked like a monstrous hedgehog. He spun toward me and bared a mouth full of nightmarish fangs. "Water for tea is boiled!"

"Thank you."

I tossed tea leaves into a small glass teapot, poured the near-boiling water from the electric kettle into it, and watched it turn golden brown. Orro found our TV fascinating. His latest discovery was the Food Channel and Garry Keys' Fire and Lightning cooking show. Garry specialized in Latin American and Mexican cuisine and when things went his way while cooking, he'd shout "Fire and Lightning!"

Orro had shortened it to "Fire!" which he yelled at surprising moments, giving Gertrude Hunt kittens.

I poured my tea into a cup and sipped it. Mmmm…. Thirteen days ago, the siege of the inn had finally ended, and we'd celebrated Christmas, a full week late, on New Year's Day. Tomorrow, on January 14th, we would celebrate Treaty Stay, the oldest of the innkeeper holidays. You could skip Christmas and forget Thanksgiving, but no inn ever failed to celebrate Treaty Stay. Hopefully we'd still have the inn to celebrate in. If everything went according to plan, tonight we'd leave for Casa Feliz, a large inn in Dallas where we would attend an Assembly meeting and answer uncomfortable questions…

Tony walked into the kitchen. Tall, tan, and dark haired, Tony Rodriguez gave the impression of being harmless. Sometimes he looked sleepy and slightly befuddled. Sometimes, especially around his father, Brian Rodriguez, who ran Casa Feliz, he wore the "grant me patience" expression instantly recognizable by any adult child who had to endure lectures on the wrongfulness of their life choices. The prospect of tasting Orro's culinary masterpieces reduced Tony to excited giddiness.

Some of it had to be a front, because Tony was an ad-hal, the Assembly's guardian and enforcer of its judgements. But most of it was genuine Tony. And right now, Tony looked like he wanted to be anywhere but here.

My stomach dropped. "What happened?"

"I have good news and bad news."

"Give me the good news."

Sean walked into the kitchen.

Tony perched on the edge of the dining room table. "The good news is that we don't have to go to my father's inn, because your appointment with the Assembly has been postponed."

Orro spun around. "I do not like this Assembly. It jerks the small human to and fro." He stabbed the air with his giant fork for emphasis. "Can they not see that she is exhausted? Do they not know what she has been through? Come to the meeting, do not come to the meeting, is there no decorum?"

"I'm not in charge of the Assembly's decisions," Tony said.

"What's the bad news?" Sean asked.

"You have a special request."

Now? "Treaty Stay?"

Tony nodded.

No innkeeper could turn away a guest during Treaty Stay unless that guest had been banned from the inns. The Treaty Stay didn't start for another twenty-four hours, but the Assembly had cancelled our meeting, which meant they thought I would require these twenty-four hours to prepare... Oh no.

"A Drífan?"

Orro sucked in an audible breath. Tony nodded.

"Are you serious?"

He nodded for the third time.

During the fight with the clan of assassins who had besieged our inn, the leader of the assassins sent me a seed, a little baby inn, too weak to survive. I had jumped through a dimensional gateway to keep its death from injuring Gertrude Hunt, but living through it had rendered me unresponsive. Gertrude Hunt had survived several days without me. If it hadn't been for my sister and my niece, the inn would have gone mad or turned catatonic. It'd been thirteen days and as I moved around the inn, Gertrude Hunt watched me. The inn was always aware of me, but now it had redoubled its efforts. If it was a person, it would be hovering over my shoulder, terrified that I might stumble and it would miss the opportunity to catch me.

And now the Assembly wanted me to host a Drífan.

"Is it a liege?" I asked. "Please don't nod again."

"Yes," Tony said.

Perfect. Just perfect.

Orro spun around and hurled a cabbage at Tony's head. Tony caught it and set it on the table. "Again, I'm just the messenger."

I sighed and poured more tea. This was fundamentally unfair.

"I swear, it's not a punishment."

"Who are the Drífan?" Sean asked.

"Drífan is singular," I told him. "Drífen is plural. The first comprehensive account of them was given by an Anglo-Saxon innkeeper and we are stuck with a lot of Old English terms which we have since butchered. Drífan is a very old word. It means to drive, to force living beings to move, to cause one to flee before one's pursuit, to chase, to hunt, to force by a blow, to proceed with violence."

"Okay," Sean said. "None of those are good."

"The Drífen are probably the most magical beings in the galaxy," Tony explained. "Their star system is only accessible through a dimensional rip. They are magic, the star system is magic, and their planets are very choosy about who they allow to enter and leave. We don't know very much about them. We do know that there are several states within the star system and they may or may not be at war with each other."

"The states are ruled by emperors," I added. "The emperors rely on a vast bureaucracy and liege lords, dryhten, for power. Each liege lord is responsible for a dryht, a combination of a clan, a sect, and a magic order. The dryht exists in a magical symbiosis with the territory it occupies, and its members take on the characteristics of whatever their dryht is dedicated to."

"So, if the dryht is dedicated to an animal predator, they develop a better sense of smell and grow claws?" Sean asked.

"Sometimes." I drank more tea. Right now, I'd need an ocean of tea to make me feel better. "For example, if we had to host a person from a Fire Dryht, we would have to make special quarters for them as far away from the main building as we could, because Gertrude Hunt would think that they were literally living fire and would try to douse them. The inns intensely dislike the Drífen. Their magic scares them, especially if they are from a dryht that's dedicated to a landscape or a plant. The inns, at their cores, are trees."

Sean turned to Tony. "Which dryht are we hosting?"

Tony took a deep breath.

Please don't be a regional dryht, please don't be a regional dryht. I would take an element, a mineral, an animal...

"Green Mountain."

I groaned.

"I'm sorry." Tony raised his hands.

Sean looked to me.

"Green Mountain is called that because it's covered with trees," I said. "It's one of the worst for us."

"Can we decline?"

I shook my head.

"You could," Tony said. "But the liege specifically requested this inn and no guest, unless they have been banned already, can be turned away from an inn for the duration of the Treaty Stay."

"It's worse than that," I told Sean. "The Treaty Stay is the anniversary of the three days when the Treaty of Earth was written into being. The inns had existed before that, but not in an official capacity. On the first day of the Treaty Stay, the oldest inns in China, the Kingdom of Aksum, the Satavahana Empire, Rome, the three inns in the Americas, and the lands of the Northern Venedae hosted representatives of different galactic civilizations. Each inn had three guests, each from a different species: a warrior, a sage, and a pilgrim. One of the warrior guests was a Drífan. Their name is on the original treaty."

"If you absolutely kick your feet and refuse, Casa Feliz will step in," Tony said. "But I wouldn't recommend it."

Caldenia swept into the room. Her Grace had elevated the idea of aging gracefully to an art. She wore a deep-green robe of shimmering silk. Her grey hair curled on top of her head in an elegant wave, studded with emeralds and dripping with platinum filigree. Her makeup was subtle and flawless, accentuating her cheek bones and brightening her skin. It did nothing to diminish the predatory light in her eyes.

"Why the sour faces?" she asked.

"The Assembly meeting has been cancelled. We're hosting a Drífan liege instead," I told her.

"Which dryht?"

"Green Mountain."

Caldenia shrugged. "I have no doubt you will rise to the challenge, my dear. Or were you thinking of declining?"

"Gertrude Hunt honors our Treaty Stay obligations," I told her. "As you well know."

"Excellent. Life gives us precious few opportunities to put our best foot forward, so when a chance to shine presents itself, one should always take it." Caldenia grinned, baring inhumanely sharp teeth. "Besides, it's been almost two weeks since anyone was brutally murdered. Things were getting a bit dull. We wouldn't want to die of boredom, would we?"

THE OFFICIAL COLORS OF TREATY STAY WERE GREEN AND PASTEL lavender, closer to pink than to purple, because the first inn to receive the three visitors for the ceremonial signing of the treaty was located in China and the innkeeper, hoping to impress the guests, coaxed the foxglove trees on the grounds to bloom.

I surveyed the Grand Ballroom and waved my broom. The glowing nebulae on the ceiling turned pink, lavender, and white against the cosmos. The enormous light fixtures suspended from the ceiling withdrew. New green stems of pale metal spiraled out, braiding into a canopy around the columns, and sprouted glass flowers a full two feet across. The foxglove tree blooms started purple at the base of the flute, then paled at the tips of the frilly petals. The flowers shivered and opened, revealing glowing yellow centers and dark purple dotted lines running down the length of the delicate flutes. Pastel-colored lanterns appeared in the canopy, bathing the room in a soft light. Matching banners unrolled on the walls that had turned sage green. I turned the color of the columns to a deep red and surveyed the room.

Good. The floor didn't match though.

Fatigue rolled over me. Tinting the floor mosaic would take a lot of magic.

I sat down with my back against the nearest column. Beast, my little black-and-white Shih Tzu, trotted over to me and flopped at my feet. I scratched her tummy.

Tony left back to Casa Feliz, his father's inn. I'd spent most of the day making rooms for the Drífan. Or Drífen. In my experience beings in position of power rarely travelled alone. I had stripped the Otrokar wing of its decorations, since we wouldn't be expecting a large delegation from the Hope-Crushing Horde any time soon, and repurposed the space. Sean spent the day cataloging the damages to our defenses. Fighting with a clan of interstellar assassins had taken a toll, and he had gone through the garage looking for tools and ended up pulling spare parts out of storage. I'd passed him on the stairs a few times, as he carried various odd-looking doohickeys a normal human shouldn't have been able to lift. At some point he went to repair the particle cannon on the west side, and I heard him cursing in three different languages while I reshaped the balcony.

It was evening now, and I was tired. The fight with the Draziri damaged more than just our guns. Living through the death of the baby inn was like entering a comatose state, except I had been aware of everything that was happening. Breaking out of it was the hardest thing I had ever done in my life. I still felt…depleted somehow. And the inn wasn't responding as readily as I was used to. It didn't exactly hesitate, but the connection between us was slightly muddled. Maybe I could do the mosaic first thing in the morning.

Sean walked into the Grand Ballroom. He'd traded the robe for his usual jeans and T-shirt. There was something wolfish about Sean Evans even in his human form. It was the way he moved, with a deceptively leisurely stride, or the way he held himself, ready, or maybe it was in his eyes. Sometimes when I looked into them, a wolf gazed back at me from the edges of a dark forest.

He approached and smoothly sat on the floor next to me. Beast immediately crawled in his lap.

"I can't find anything on the Drífen in the archives," he said. "I've read Wictred's account in the inn's files and looked through the books, but there is nothing since that. Is there a code word I don't know?"

"No. There simply isn't that much information available about them."

"Usually there are notations by other innkeepers," he said.

I raised my eyebrows.

"I read a lot when you weren't yourself. The inn helped me to look for a cure."

Poor Gertrude Hunt. Poor Sean. I could picture him sitting in the room searching for the answer while the inn pulled up one archive after another. I had to make sure this didn't happen again.

"You're right," I told him. "When an innkeeper learns something new about a particular species, they will add notations to the general files. In old times, they would write entries in the books. That's why the margins are so wide. But with the Drífen, it's different. The original guidance the innkeepers received was to safeguard their privacy at all costs. In addition, each Drífan is different. There are hundreds of dryhts. You can live for a hundred years and never see two Drífen from the same dryht. Actually, you can live for a hundred years and never meet a Drífan at all."

"So, what do we do?"

"Usually the lieges will send someone ahead with their demands. We will try to get as much information as we can and go from there."

A soft melodious sound rolled through the inn. Hmm. Someone was requesting a vacancy in advance. Usually the guests simply showed up. The inn always had a vacancy, because I could make as many rooms as the guests required.

"Let me see," I told the inn.

The ceiling parted and a folded parchment fell into my hands. Sean raised his eyebrows.

"The innkeeper before me died in the 1980s," I explained. "He was solitary, a bit odd, and overly fond of antiques. A lot of Gertrude Hunt's communication happened on parchment when I got here. I fixed most of it, but once in a while something like this happens. In the future, a screen would be fine."

I opened the parchment and read it. Just what we needed. This was shaping up to be a hell of a holiday. I passed the parchment to Sean.

He glanced at it. "A family dispute, party of sixty-one?"

13

"It looks like two sides of the same family have descended from two brothers. One of them left and founded an influential philosophy school on a different planet, while the other remained on the home world and established his own philosophical academy. Now they are feuding about which of the brothers can truly be considered the family's founder: the one who left to colonize the new planet or the one who stayed on their original world. They've invited a wise elder to settle their dispute."

"Sixty-one new guests. Seems like it would be good for the inn, but you don't look happy."

"They are koo-ko."

Sean looked at the ceiling. "Show me a koo-ko."

A screen slid from the wall. On it, a being about thirty inches tall spread its plumage. Soft cream feathers covered its face, brightening to a shocking pink on the back of its head and back and turning vivid crimson on the wings and bushy tail. A second pair of appendages that resembled the front limbs of a dinosaur or perhaps a monkey if the monkey somehow grew talons, thrust from underneath the wings.

An oversized tail marked the koo-ko as a male. He wore an elaborate pleated harness that fit over his head and sat on his shoulders, then widened into a lavish utility belt stuffed with electronics, quills made from bright feathers, and rolls of something suspiciously resembling toilet paper on a wide bobbin.

The koo-ko looked at us with purple eyes, fluffed up his feathers, and strode back and forth, his plump body rocking with each step.

Sean cracked a smile. "They are chickens."

"Technically they're not even avian."

"Dina, we're going to host sixty-one space chickens."

I gave up. "Yes."

"And they're going to argue philosophy."

"Mhm. This means they will want a forum with a podium and a debate circle, and a coop to sleep in, and we have to buy a lot of grain..."

He laughed.

"You're not taking this very seriously."

"We'll have to tell Orro to stop serving poultry."

"Sean Evans!"

He put his arm around me. I leaned against him.

"A beautiful room," he said.

It was beautiful. There was something ethereal about the Treaty Stay, something fresh and clean and hopeful, like a bright spring day after a terrible winter.

"You've hosted a peace summit between the Holy Anocracy, the Merchants and the Hope-Crushing Horde. And then you took on the Draziri," Sean said.

"Yes."

"I've never seen you this anxious. What's the matter?"

I sighed.

"Is it the Assembly?"

"Partially. I don't like not knowing where we stand with them, but in the end, as you said, they can only downgrade us. They can't take away Gertrude Hunt unless we commit a truly heinous offense."

"So, it's the Drífan."

"I abandoned my inn." It just kind of fell out.

Sean frowned. "I don't follow."

"When I jumped through the door with the seed of the baby Inn, I abandoned Gertrude Hunt. The inn had to survive without me. I traumatized it."

"You had no choice."

"I know. But the inn is fragile now. It waits and watches and the connection between us...is more tentative. I don't know if

Gertrude Hunt is afraid of getting hurt or of me being hurt, or maybe it worries it might hurt me somehow. But there is a distance between us. It wasn't noticeable day-to-day, but redecorating the inn for the Treaty Stay is complicated and requires precision. I feel it, and now that I'm aware of it, it worries me. Adding a Drífan on top of it's too much..."

The floor in the back of the Grand Ballroom parted. That's where I had put the massive Christmas tree before. Gertrude Hunt was doing something...

"We'll take it day by day," Sean said.

Something rumbled underneath the floor. A massive foxglove tree emerged from the depths of the inn, spreading huge branches through the ballroom. The long tree limbs dripped flower buds, still closed but tipped with faint lavender. I had no idea Gertrude Hunt had that hidden away. The inn didn't show it to me the last two Treaty Stays. But then we had barely celebrated. Hard to be excited about holidays when you know your inn will be empty.

"Wow," Sean said.

"That's why they call it the Empress tree. Wait until it blooms."

Magic tugged on me. Someone had crossed the boundary of the inn.

"Back camera."

Gertrude Hunt tossed the video feed from the back camera onto the screen. A tall man strode through the back field toward the inn. A two-tone cloak, dark green on one side and black on the other, wrapped his shoulders, elaborately draped and secured with an ornate metal pin in the shape of a dagger. The metal of the pin shone faintly as he walked. He wore a complex layered robe, charcoal and accented with bright green, and carried a long staff tipped with three claws. The claws clutched a blue jewel the size of a medium apple. Two blades curved around the jewel, turning the staff into a halberd. A deep hood hid his head.

A small creature about three feet tall walked by him, holding on to his cloak with a dark brown raccoon hand. Fuzzy with cream and brown fur, it moved upright on two legs, the fur dense and thick on its body, but slicker and darker below its knees and elbows. A long fluffy tail curled into a squirrel-like S behind it. Its head was round, with a short dark muzzle and an adorable cat nose. Its eyes were round too, and huge, glowing with pale yellow when they caught the fading light. Its ears were layered, frilly and trembling, pointing downward like two floppy flowers on the sides of its head. As it walked, it must've heard a noise, because its ears snapped upright and it froze, terrified, standing on one skinny foot, its tail fluffed out so the fur stood on end like spikes.

The person in the cloak kept walking.

The small creature shook, seemingly torn, dashed after him, and clutched at the hem of his cloak again.

The Drífan's representative had arrived.

[2]

S ean met the Drífan by the door. It swung open in front of
him without me having to ask Gertrude Hunt, which made
me ridiculously happy. He gave the guest a one-second look and
stepped aside, inviting the Drífan to enter. The cloaked person
stepped into the sitting room.

"Welcome to Gertrude Hunt," I said. I decided that meeting
him in the front room was the best strategy. The less time he had
to spend in the inn, the better.

The Drífan inclined his head. The small creature by his feet
looked ready to faint from stress.

"Please sit."

A smooth voice issued forth from under the hood. "I shall
stand."

I sat on the couch. Orro loomed in the doorway to the kitchen
on my left, while Caldenia perched in a padded chair by the
window on the far right, sipping her tea and pretending to not be
a part of this.

The guest drew back his hood. The same set of genes that gave
rise to humans, vampires, and Otrokars had spread far through

the galaxy, but one look at the Drífan, and you knew this wasn't a sibling, but a distant cousin at best. His otherness slapped you in the face.

His face was all angles, lacking the human softness. His nose was sharply cut, just like his cheekbones, and his nostrils resembled that of a cat rather than a human. Light and dark patterns colored his walnut-brown skin, the kind you would see on a piece of polished red agate. They weren't tattooed on or drawn; instead they seemed to be a natural pigmentation of his epidermis. His wide amber eyes glowed slightly with an eerie light, and the hand holding his staff had long, amber-colored claws. His hair, straight and loose, fell in a grey curtain around his face. He was beardless, but long grey whiskers hung from his upper lip.

"Greetings, innkeeper," the Drífan said in a melodious voice.

"Greetings, herald of Dryhten." And I had just exhausted the knowledge of the Drífen pleasantries from Wictred's account. We were on our own. "My name is Dina Demille. The man by the door is Sean Evans."

The Drífan nodded slowly. "Call me Zedas. My mistress, who is without equal, she whose heart beats with the power of a mountain waterfall, she who is resolute like the sun, elegant like the moon, unyielding like living stone, yet versatile like a stream of pure water dashing about the rocks, she who kills enemies by the thousands, she who shelters her friends, who is feared by warriors, respected by scholars, beloved by her dryht, and recognized by the Emperor, sends you her greetings."

"Cool," Sean said.

I threw him a warning glance. "We are honored."

"You are blessed, for she has chosen this humble inn for her visit to this realm. I'm here to show you the inner sights of her lodge so she may be comfortable in her time of hardship. Look well, innkeeper, for your eyes will see a sight not witnessed by one of your kind in hundreds of years."

Zedas spun the staff and drew it in a wide circle. A ripple followed it as if the air had become liquid. The space between us shimmered and a holographic projection of startling clarity appeared in the sitting room. A throne room with a raised dais supported a crude throne chipped out of soft, translucent white stone saturated with veins of crimson, so dense in places, they had turned it blood red. The carving was so primitive, it looked almost prehistoric. I would have guessed a very high-quality chicken blood jade, but that stone's red color came from cinnabar. Cinnabar darkened to brown with exposure to light. The ancient throne sat bathed in the light from the window, and the veins were vivid and bright.

Everything else around the throne spoke of artisan craftsmanship and restrained opulence. The floor resembled a river, with alternating ribbons of malachite and onyx the color of warm honey flowing from the dais toward the walls. Wooden columns, square and elaborately carved, rose from the floor. The wood was unstained but heavily patterned, reminiscent of acacia sealed with a clear coat of resin. The walls matched the columns, interrupted by ornate stone reliefs, delicate metal screens depicting strange birds and animals with jeweled eyes, and paintings almost ethereal in their simplicity.

The view moved, as the carrier of the camera walked through a tall doorway to an outside balcony that wrapped all the way around the building under a protruding roof. Here the floor was polished grey stone, bordered by a matching stone balustrade. Stone columns supported a high eave. Beyond the balcony was an ocean of air. Far below, small mountains rose, cushioned with trees that from this height resembled emerald green moss. A huge bird soared on the air currents, a hybrid of an eagle and a condor, its plumage a dark shade of sapphire. It looked large enough to carry off a human.

The projection vanished.

"I trust this is sufficient," the herald said.

So many little details that had to be perfect. No two panels or columns matched, and the patterns were meticulous. This would be a ton of work, and we didn't get to see a bedroom either. For all we knew, they slept in nests.

"It is," I said. "How many beings will accompany your liege?"

"Myself and four others."

Crap. I had to make extra rooms. "What are the dietary preferences of your mistress?"

"She prefers vegetables and fruit, cooked lightly or not at all, cold-water fish cooked well, and red meat served rare. For her first meal, she has a special request. There are no equivalent words in our language, and my mouth is old and set in its ways, so I cannot shape the sounds. I have brought this small one to speak it for me."

He nodded at the furry thing. It shrunk back, but Zedas looked at it. The furry creature stepped forward, clutching its hands into a single fist. The pinkie finger on its left hand was missing, the stump ragged, as if it had been sawed off. It caught me looking and curled its hands into fists.

"Go on," Zedas said.

The furry beast opened its mouth and a clear voice that should have belonged to some cute Muppet issued forth. "A double Grand Burger with cheese, large fries, and a Coke."

You could have knocked me over with a feather.

"Was the pronunciation satisfactory?" Zedas asked.

"It was," I managed.

Zedas motioned with his hand. The furry beast scampered

forward and held out a scrap of paper to me with trembling hands.

"Thank you." I took the paper. On it written in ink in beautiful calligraphy were the words "Rudolph Peterson" along with a sequence of numbers that had to belong to a US phone.

The little creature dashed back and hid behind Zedas, clutching the cloak and holding the fabric like a shield between itself and us. He ignored it.

"My mistress is gracing your inn with her presence and is willing to endure the adversity of travel so she can meet this person. He has requested this meeting and in her infinite grace, she condescended to grant it. You will inform this person tomorrow that his presence is required here on the last day of the Treaty Stay, 5:00 p.m., and you will provide my mistress with a secure location for this meeting. Should he be late, she will not wait for him. Should he be early, she will not see him before the appointed time." Zedas looked at the beast again. "Time for your second message."

The creature lowered the cloak so only its face was visible, looking at us with huge freaked out eyes. Clear English words spilled out. "Rudolph Peterson is an evil man and he's not to be trusted."

"Did you understand?" Zedas asked.

"We understand perfectly," Sean said.

"Then my mission here is complete," Zedas announced. "I shall return with my mistress in one day and night cycle. Prepare well, innkeeper."

———

I WATCHED THE HERALD AND THE SMALL CREATURE DISAPPEAR AT

the edge of the inn's boundary. One moment they were there and the next they simply vanished.

"Interesting," Caldenia raised her cup to her lips and sipped her tea. "That was an Akeraat, my dear. An old one, too."

She'd pronounced all three a's the way u was pronounced in cup. I rummaged through my memory and came up with a blank. "I'm not familiar with that one."

"They are very rare. They occupy a single planet on the proximal end of the galaxy's central bar. The place looks like a ball of crumpled paper—mountains and valleys with narrow seas in between. Predictably, the geography nudged their culture toward the formation of numerous city-states that exist in continuous conflict."

"No larger countries?" Sean asked.

"No. Sometimes several cities are conquered and bound into a single realm, but it doesn't last. Their resources are relatively equally distributed, and they don't trust each other. Akeraats plot. It's their national pastime, sport, and merit competition. They spy on each other, form alliances then stab their allies in the back, poison rival leaders and their own, and engineer the rise and fall of dynasties." Caldenia smiled like a shark. "They are great fun."

I shuddered.

"They're very sought out as counselors and advisors, but they're extremely reluctant to leave their planet. Luring one away is a huge boon." Caldenia lowered her eyelashes. "Naturally, I had one."

"What happened?" Sean asked.

"He was marvelous until the rebels assassinated him."

Of course.

Sean was looking at his phone. His face told me that he didn't like what he saw.

"What are you looking at?" I asked.

"Rudolph Peterson. He has his own Wikipedia entry."

"What does it say?"

"'Rudolph Peterson is the chairman and chief executive officer of the Peterson group, a diversified holding company with assets in oil, shipping, real estate development, and private equity.' Wikipedia puts his worth between 50 and 100 million."

"So a Drífan liege is coming here to meet a multi-millionaire who is an evil man and is not to be trusted and she wants a quarter pounder for dinner." I exhaled, blowing the air out slowly.

"That sums it up." Sean looked at me. "How secure are you in the real world, Dina?"

"What do you mean?"

"Do you own the land the inn sits on?"

"I own the land and the twenty-three acres behind it. Everything behind the inn is mine."

"Is it a mortgage?"

"No, Sean. The original six-acre parcel was an Assembly grant. It's ironclad. I bought the eight acres directly behind us after Caldenia moved in, and the other nine acres, to the side and behind the inn after the peace summit. I own it outright; there is no mortgage."

"Good." His face didn't seem any brighter. "I'm going to call Marais."

He walked outside.

I drummed my fingers on the armrest of the chair. "The little creature spoke English like an American. Specifically, like a Southern American. Burgeh. Trahsted."

"So you feel his liege also speaks that way." Caldenia frowned. "How could an American end up as a Drífan liege?"

"I don't know." There were so many facets to this puzzle.

"What is this Grand Burger?" Orro demanded from the doorway.

I almost jumped. He'd been so quiet, I forgot he was there.

"It's a hamburger from Burger Feast, a fast-food chain," Sean told him, coming back inside. That was fast. He must've gotten voicemail.

"I have seen it on your TV. Bring it to me and I will make it."

I sighed. "Orro, if this person comes from Earth, from our country, the Grand Burger likely has a sentimental value to her. She will want the entire experience, the burger, the fries, the Coke. It's a cheap meal, unworthy of your talent. It's best to just buy it for her."

Orro drew himself to his full height. "You want to bring outside food into my kitchen?"

Oh no.

"Am I not a Red Cleaver chef?"

And here we go.

"Have I not cooked delicacies from a thousand planets?"

His quills stood straight up. He raised his right hand, his talons spread wide, appealing to heavens. "Am I not a master of my craft?"

He paused, glaring at me.

"Of course you are," I said, trying to keep my voice soothing. This would end in disaster.

"Then you will bring this Grand Burger to me and I shall make it. You will taste it and you will weep, for it will be the best Grand Burger to ever grace a human mouth."

He spun around dramatically and stalked off into the kitchen.

"We should get him a cape," Sean said.

[3]

T*ing. Ting.*
 A soft, insistent chime fought its way through my sleep. I was so warm and comfy. My pillow was soft, my blanket was like a cloud, and Sean's strong hot arm was wrapped around my waist.

Ting. Ting.

Mmm. I scooted closer to Sean. So warm…

TING. TING.

I opened my eyes. A small screen hovered about four inches in front of my face. A small indicator blinked in the corner in pale green: 05:00. The back field, all dead grass and weeds; the sky still dark but beginning to lighten; the ripple in the fabric of existence hanging horizontally about three feet from the ground…

I jerked upright in the bed. Sean grabbed me, pulled me back, and vaulted over me to land on the carpet, a wicked green knife in his hand. He scanned the room, poised on his toes, keeping himself between me and the threat.

Wow.

"What is it?" Sean asked, his voice a low growl.

"The koo-ko!" I scrambled off the bed, sprinting for my robe hanging on a hook.

"They aren't due until tonight."

I pulled my robe on. "They're fifteen hours early."

Thirty seconds later, I tore out of the inn onto the back porch. Cold bit at my bare legs under the robe. I barely had time to pull the robe over my sleeping T-shirt. My nose was freezing. I wore small lavender crocs with fuzzy lining in them, which I used as house slippers, because that was all I could find on short notice. Next to me, Sean stood in his own copper robe.

The ripple had widened, pulsating, as if an invisible bobber was dancing on the air.

"Do you always sleep with a knife?" I murmured.

"Yes."

Pointing out that he had nothing to fear inside Gertrude Hunt wouldn't do any good. He knew it already. Another scar from Nexus. It would get better with time. At least I hoped it would.

A yellow light burst in the center of the ripple and a rotund feathered body popped up above it, as if shot out from an underground cannon. The koo-ko spread his russet wings, suspended for a fraction of a second, his big purple eyes opened wide, and landed on the ground with a squawk, his feathers erect, his leather apron slightly askew.

Sean swore.

Another koo-ko shot out, then another, and another, two at a time, as if a koo-ko geyser had sprouted in our backyard. The koo-ko sorted themselves into two roughly equal groups, those with mostly reddish and pink plumage and those with pale lavender and green. Finally, an older, almost completely white koo-ko popped free of the ripple and landed in front of the two groups. Two younger koo-ko's, with turquoise feathers, flanked him on both sides. The left koo-ko handed him an elaborately carved cane. The right koo-ko held out a complex headdress of twisted metal wire, studded with gems, and plonked it on the elder's head, buckling the chin strap in place.

The elder drew himself to his full height, which was about three feet, three and a half if you counted the hat, adjusted his headdress before it slid off his head, and strode toward us.

"Greetings, innkeeper. Greetings, tiercel."

He must have used a term for a male in a military role, but his implant ended up mangling it. If Sean was surprised by being addressed as a male falcon, he didn't show it.

I nodded. "Greetings, venerable First Scholar. We expected you this evening."

The koo-ko elder cleared his throat. "Yes, well, ahem, we would have arrived this evening if certain boisterous members didn't open a debate on the lack of virtue in those who arrive late."

"If you're not fifteen minutes early, you're late," Sean said.

The elder pointed his wing at Sean. "Exactly! In this discussion of how early is early enough, nobody wanted to be later than their opponent, therefore when the debate reached its sixth hour, the discussion had to be cut short so everyone could transit before feathers started flying. I do apologize on behalf of my brethren. I trust our quarters are in order?"

Thank the galaxy that I had spent a good chunk of yesterday making their coops. "Of course they are. Follow me, please."

I stepped through the door. The elder and his two assistants followed. The two groups of koo-ko lined up in two columns, two abreast, and tried to enter the inn simultaneously. The two columns bumped into each other. There was outraged glaring and mild shoving, followed by raised feathers. Neither group showed any inclination to let the other go first. Clearly, the zipper merging maneuver wasn't their strong suit.

I widened the doorway. The koo-ko on the edges stumbled, suddenly unstuck, righted themselves, and marched forward, beaks in the air, ignoring each other. This would be a fun visit.

The inn scanned them as they went through the doorway. I put only one condition on hosting this debate: no weapons. No alarms blared. The koo-ko were clean.

I led them deeper into the inn, past the portrait of my missing parents. None of the koo-ko had any reaction to it. One day someone would recognize my mother and father, and then nothing would stop me from finding them.

We marched down the long hallway to a door. It swung open

at my approach and we walked into a large, well-lit chamber. In the center, rows of benches faced each other, three on each side, arranged like bleachers with the furthest bench from the center being the highest. Between the benches lay an open space with a single podium. A large, throne-like chair faced the podium, edged by two smaller chairs, one for each of the elder's assistants.

At the opposite ends of the chamber, two large koo-ko coops waited, raised off the ground the traditional five feet, with a bathroom section on the far end and two baths, one water, the other fine heated sand, in front. A thirty-foot-wide indoor channel filled with water separated each coop from the amphitheater, spanned by an arched bridge.

Like many sentient winged species, the koo-ko lost the power of flight when their brains and dexterity became more important. Wings didn't help one manipulate tools or perform mathematical calculations. But the koo-ko could still glide and leap great distances. A typical leap for a koo-ko was about twenty feet and they hated swimming. The prospect of landing in the water would make even the most reckless koo-ko think twice.

I pointed my broom at a luxurious coop directly behind the amphitheater. "Your personal accommodations, First Scholar. The two bridges retract. The inn will listen only to you, and if you wish, you can withdraw the bridges as the need arises. Simply say 'fold' and you can keep the two groups separated. Say 'unfold' to extend the bridges again. Please try it now."

The First Scholar cleared his throat and waved his right wing. "Fold."

The bridges retracted.

"Unfold. Fold. Unfold. Very good."

The elder surveyed the channels and coops. "They are exactly the same?"

"Identical."

"Good, good, good. Separate but equal. Thank you, innkeeper."

"Breakfast and all of your meals will be served here. We ask that you remain in this chamber at all times for your safety. We are expecting a Drífan liege."

The elder whipped his head around to look at me and his headdress nearly fell. One of his assistants jumped up and slid it back into place.

"Understood," the elder said. "I shall keep my flock contained."

"Should you need anything, call my name and the inn will put you in contact with me. I'm called Dina."

"Very well, Dina. I'm called…well, it's really too long. Please call me First Scholar Thek." He raised his voice. "Come, students of thought. Let us find our comfort."

The koo-kos streamed around me, heading straight for the amphitheater.

I bowed my head and escaped.

From the hallway, Sean watched me beat a strategic retreat. The door slid shut behind me and I leaned against the hallway wall.

"Got them settled?"

"Sort of. We won't know if the coops are adequate until this evening."

He raised his eyebrows.

"It will take them that long to debate who takes which identical coop." I started down the hallway. There was no sleeping now. I'd get a strong cup of tea and work on the Drífan palace quarters.

"When do you want to call the evil millionaire?" he asked.

"I don't know. It's an east coast number. Around ten?"

"I want to be there."

"Okay," I promised and kissed him.

THE FIRST BATCH OF TEN GRAND BURGERS ARRIVED AT 6:15 A.M., AS soon as we could get them. Unlike most fast-food chains that delayed burger grills until 10:00 a.m. or so because they served breakfast items, Burger Feast would give you a hamburger any time, day or night.

Orro had studied the collection of burgers the way a hunter studied prey. His long sensitive nose had twitched. He'd unwrapped one, moving his scary claws with surgical precision to peel off the trademark orange and purple wrapper, raised the burger to his eye level, evaluated the meat, took off the bun, looked at the patty smothered in the special sauce, put the bun back on, and finally took a bite.

Silence.

Orro chewed.

More silence.

He'd turned around and spat the burger into the garbage disposal. "She wants this?"

"Apparently."

"This isn't food. This is a crime against the art of cooking."

It was 9:50 a.m. now, and Orro had produced his seventh burger, the first he deemed good enough for me to try. It rested on a plate now, waiting for my verdict.

I took a bite. Oh my galaxy.

Orro hovered over me. "Well?"

"Mmmhghpph." I swallowed. "It's the best hamburger I've ever had."

"But does it taste like the Grand Burger?"

"No. It tastes better."

He snatched the hamburger back.

"Orro!"

The hamburger hurtled through the room into the garbage bin. I almost cried.

"I do not understand how they achieve this unnatural texture," he murmured. "Or why anyone would eat it."

"It's a fast, cheap meal. It tastes delicious when you're hungry."

"Callowinian spider squids also taste delicious when one is hungry, but that doesn't mean one should bring oneself to cook them."

I had no idea what callowinian spider squids tasted like or why it was a bad idea to cook them, but now was the perfect time to talk him out of his burger quest. "As I said, this is a meal unworthy of your skill. It's beneath you."

He drew himself to his full height. His chest expanded.

Oh no.

"I shall duplicate it! Perfectly!"

"Orro..."

"FIRE!"

He spun around. The inn opened the pantry door for him, and Orro vanished into the pocket within reality to look for the ingredients.

I rubbed my face. Sean walked through the doorway and landed in a chair next to me, brushing his hand over my shoulder on his way there.

"Didn't work?" he murmured.

"Fire," I told him.

"That good, huh?"

"I'm on a tiny planet, and there is a comet heading my way and I can't do anything about it." I picked up the phone. "Ready?"

"Ready."

I dialed the number. It rang once, twice...

"Yes?" a clipped male voice said into the phone. The man sounded too young to be Rudolph.

"I have a message for Mr. Rudolph Peterson."

"Go ahead."

"Are you Mr. Peterson?"

"I will deliver your message."

"I would prefer to speak to him."

"That's not possible."

I glanced at Sean. He nodded. We didn't exactly have a choice.

"Tell him that the meeting he's been waiting for will take place on January 16th at 5:00 p.m. Central time at the following address." I gave him the address for Gertrude Hunt. "The time window for this visit's very short. He must not be late, or he will miss her."

"Understood."

The man hung up. Well, that's that.

"I looked into Peterson," Sean said.

"What did you find out?"

"He is an asshole."

"Okay. Strong statement, but not informative."

Sean leaned back. "He made his money in real estate. He started as an agent and moved into being a builder. When the housing crisis happened, a lot of builders went out of business, and he bought their equipment and the land they were stuck with, dirt cheap. He also hired most of his competitors as project managers complete with their work force. His people spun it as him being a hero, giving the out-of-work tradesmen a chance to put food on the table. In reality, he locked them into restrictive contracts with non-competes, making him effectively the only builder in several key markets in Arizona, Colorado, and Utah. In some cases, wages haven't been paid, and benefits weren't granted. When people complained, he fired them. If they continued to complain, he would drag them to court. He's a big believer in NDAs."

"This sounds worse and worse."

"An Arizona newspaper did an article on him, and he filed a SLAPP suit. It dragged on for three years. The newspaper eventually won, but the suit took so long, they went bankrupt meanwhile and had to close. By that point he'd expanded into other businesses. New song, same dance—he goes after failing enterprises, grabs them cheap, and then cashes in on their desperation."

I didn't like any of this. Rudolph Peterson sounded like the kind of man who would make trouble, and I wanted to avoid trouble at all costs. I already had my hands full.

"Do not worry," Orro said, emerging from the pantry and cold storage with a heap of groceries in his arms. "If this human creates problems, we will feed him the Grand Burgers. Once he consumes enough of them, his body will surely fail."

If only it were that easy.

———

I'd spent the entire morning refining the Drífen rooms. The distance between me and Gertrude Hunt kept getting in the way. I felt it every time I needed to do something elaborate. It was like trying to do an intricate drawing with a blunted pencil. I could make the inn do what I wanted it to do, but it required a lot of concentration and occasional do-overs.

I had never in my life experienced anything like this. I was born in an inn; for all of my life it had been a constant presence, a third parent, always ready to catch me if I stumbled. Yesterday, I'd read some of the innkeeper diaries Gertrude Hunt had stored in its database, looking for someone having a problem with my symptoms. I found nothing. The distance was there, and the more I felt it, the closer I edged to panic.

I couldn't tell if it was getting better or worse. In the end, I sat down on the ornamental staircase to catch a breath and rested, feeling Gertrude Hunt around me.

"It's alright." I stroked the stairs with my fingertips. "We will figure it out. Don't worry. I'm not going anywhere."

That's where Sean found me.

He came through the doorway with measured grace, no wasted movement, no deviation from the course, and headed straight for me. Beast trailed him, making happy snorting noises.

He sat next to me and looked at my handiwork. "Beautiful."

"Thank you. How are the weapon systems?"

"Deadly." He sank a ton of sarcasm into that one word.

"Really?"

"No. The northern particle cannon is trashed. One of the Draziri must have sank a long-range heat burst into it. Everything's fried. The HELL units won't talk to me."

"I bought them secondhand from a Morodiak. The inn partially integrated it but if you want to run diagnostics, you have to speak its language."

"So, I have to growl at the HELL units?"

"Pretty much. I know you can growl, Sean. I've heard you do it."

His upper lip trembled in a snarl, betraying a flash of fang.

"Ooh, scary. The Morodiakian HELL units don't stand a chance."

"Are you humoring me?"

"Yep."

I leaned against him. He put his arm around me.

"We need to upgrade. Or at least repair," he said. "The stealth guns in the front are in good condition, but they're antiques. About a third of the long-range weapons that face the field are out of commission, and there is only so much I can do with bubble gum and duct tape. We need to replace them."

I had no room to argue. We'd taken a serious beating. I'd known opposing the Draziri would be expensive when I took the job but standing by while an entire species was being exterminated was beyond me.

"I'd do it again," I told him. "I'd shelter the Hiru again."

"Of course you would. And that's why I need you to open the Baha-char door for me."

"Wilmos?"

Sean nodded.

Wilmos owned a weapons shop at the galactic bazaar. He also ran mercenary crews and brokered deals between private soldiers and people who wanted to hire them. Like Sean, he was a werewolf without a planet, and he was the one who'd gotten Sean the Nexus job. And a small part of me worried that once Sean walked back through Wilmos' door, he wouldn't come back.

The anxiety pinched me, sharp and cold.

I couldn't tether Sean to the inn. If he left, he left. It would mean we weren't meant to be. I had to let it go.

Bringing the weapon systems back online was going to be pricy, and I really wanted to hold some money in reserve, in case the Drífen or the Assembly threw another curveball at us. I took a mental inventory of our funds.

Ugh.

"How much do you need?"

Sean thought it over and turned to me, a serious look on his face. "One dollar. Maybe three."

I rolled my eyes.

"I was paid well on Nexus."

"That's your money. You earned it."

"Damn right and I'll spend it as I please. Right now I'm richer than you."

"How do you know that?"

He grinned at me. "I asked the inn. It won't open the Bahachar door for me, but it gave me complete access to your finances. I could rob you blind."

"You think you can. Seriously, how much do we need?"

"I won't know until I get there. Dina, you have to decide if we're together or not."

"What does that have to do with anything?"

"If I'm going to live here, you have to let me contribute. It's fair. You're in charge of the guests, and I'm in charge of their security. This is what I do."

He was right. It was fair.

I pushed off the stairs. "I'll open a door for you. But only if you promise not to spend everything you have on upgrading the inn. You bled for that money."

"Mostly I made other people bleed for that money." A shadow crossed his face. "Now I'll use it for something good. Something I want."

We walked to the kitchen together. "Will you be home in time for dinner?"

"I'll try," he promised.

[4]

F inishing the Drífen quarters took forever. Not only did everything have to be intricate and ornate, but I'd had a hard time concentrating. I kept worrying about Sean, about the Assembly, about the Drífan coming, about Rudolph Peterson…

Magic tugged on me. Caldenia wanted my attention. I opened a small two-way screen in the nearest wall. "Yes, your Grace?"

Caldenia gazed at me. "It's three o'clock, my dear."

Three o'clock was the time when we had our afternoon tea, provided the inn wasn't under attack or filled with lifelong enemies trying to broker a fragile peace.

"I'll be right there."

I could have said no. I had too much to do and not enough time to do it. But I missed our tea, too. For months and months in the beginning, it had just been me and Caldenia at the inn, and even after Orro came to stay with us, he rarely joined us for tea. We finally convinced him to have dinner with us, but he was truly comfortable hovering in the kitchen, covertly watching our expressions as we ate his food. A couple of times I'd dared to make dinner so he could have the night off. Both times I'd aimed for simple things, like steak or roasted chicken. He ate the food and afterward awkwardly patted my shoulder or my head, whichever happened to be closer, so I'd know he didn't completely hate it. But Caldenia and I shared each other's company when it was just the two of us and I'd come to enjoy having tea with her.

In thirty seconds, I walked into the tearoom. I had made it months ago to Caldenia's specifications. She wanted to sit high and enjoy the view, so I had built a small turret off the dining room and you had to climb a short staircase to reach it. Today the stairs were a bit of a chore. Maybe I made them too steep.

Like all places her Grace occupied, the tearoom was an unapologetically luxurious, yet elegant space. The windows took up three quarters of the round room's wall space, offering a beautiful view of the Avalon subdivision directly across the road from us. I had a choice between the orchard or the street, and I picked the street, because Caldenia loved to people watch. Speculating on our neighbors' comings and goings provided her with endless entertainment, and she predicted affairs and identified divorces and firings with frightening precision. None of the people in the neighborhood realized that a former galactic tyrant observed every aspect of their lives.

I crossed the rosewood floor and joined Caldenia at a round table in the center of the room. The table was laser cut from a block of garnet mined many light-years away and Caldenia adored it. She said it reminded her of crystallized blood.

I picked up a small glass teapot, poured jasmine tea into her Grace's cup, filled my own, and sipped. Mmm, delicious.

Caldenia inhaled the aroma and delicately swallowed a tiny mouthful. For a couple of minutes there was only silence and tea, and I felt the knot in the pit of my stomach slowly unraveling.

"Fire!"

I winced.

Caldenia chuckled.

"It's not funny."

"On the contrary, it's quite amusing."

I drank more tea. "I don't know what has gotten into Orro. Usually he's dramatic but this is too much even for him. It's all declarative statements, grand pronouncements, and 'Fire!'"

Caldenia chuckled again.

"He's going to give the inn a heart attack. He never used to be this bad. I don't know what happened."

Caldenia looked at me from above the rim of her cup. "Let's just say that your ordeal took a toll on all of us, dear. When you sat there like a mannequin and your werewolf carried you everywhere while the inn was under attack, even I experienced emotional discomfort. It was fleeting, of course. I came to my senses quite quickly, but the momentary twinge was real. That creature in the kitchen is perhaps the most sensitive of all of us. It shook him badly."

I hadn't realized. I'd been so focused on everything that needed to be done and so absorbed in the simple happiness of having Sean that it never occurred to me that Orro was upset.

"You are his savior," Caldenia continued. "You found him at the lowest point of his life, living in squalor, without plan or purpose, and you rescued him and brought him here. For him and I, this inn and you provide a refuge, a home, if you will. If something were to happen to either of you, we would be adrift. It's a terrifying prospect."

"I hadn't considered that."

"Under normal circumstances, we would have some time to… what is that wonderful word? Process. Once, when I was quite young, I hired a squadron of Yako mercenaries. Vicious warriors, ferocious and merciless, clad in a natural scale armor with claws three inches long and teeth to match. Once I besieged Lorekat, they broke through the shields and slaughtered thousands. It was a meatgrinder. The street quite literally ran red with blood."

She said it with relish, the way most women who looked her age would say, "My husband took me on a cruise and there was free wine."

"After we took the city, the Yako leader informed me that they would be leaving. I offered them money, plunder, favors, but none of it made any difference. Their general informed me that the taking of life was a traumatizing occupation and now they had to restore the balance of their souls. They all had to return home, hug their spouses and hatchlings, and sit on their eggs. The Yako yearned for peace and comfort, and no riches could replace it. It taught me that for every period of stress there must be a time of rest and contemplation. This is the sole reason I'm still alive."

Wow.

"Our period of peace and contemplation was cut short. We are all coping as well as we can. I do it by drinking tea and watching the Laurents' divorce war. Orro is doing it by trying to abandon decades of culinary training so he can recreate street food of marginal quality. To each his own."

"What can I do?"

She shrugged. "Nothing at all. Just be unharmed for a little while and it will all go back to normal. The more normal you act, the quicker we will relax and lull ourselves into blissful complacency. Sentient beings are spectacular liars. We are gifted with an unparalleled ability to deny things that make our life unpleasant. We even pretend death isn't a certainty, because contemplating our own mortality drives us mad."

Normal. Very well, I could do normal.

"The Laurents are divorcing? They seemed like such a nice couple."

Caldenia's eyes sparkled. "Oh, it's sordid. Apparently, Elena decided that their marriage wasn't spicy enough and she talked Tom into joining a swinger's club."

"Tom and Elena? Down the street?" I didn't even know Red Deer had a swinger's club.

"Yes."

"Isn't she a middle school teacher?"

"And he works for FedEx." Caldenia grinned, showing her sharp teeth. "It gets better. The one unbreakable rule of the swinger's club is that nobody can fall in love and Elena, what is the term the kids use, caught feelings for the club's manager. Tom discovered this, moved out, and took the children. Now there is a divorce and a nasty custody battle."

"Really?"

"Yes. Elena and her new beau are living in the house and there are odd cars in their driveway at all times. And a van from Digital World came by and Margaret thinks she saw them bring in a bunch of cameras. She is sure that they are filming pornography."

"Shocking." Margaret lived across the street from the Laurents, and since she worked out of her house, she was always home.

"I know. A den of iniquity right under our noses. The best part is, Tom talked Margaret into letting him install cameras on her house. He is filming his old house twenty-four seven hoping to get enough ammunition to win sole custody. Margaret gave me her password and I can pop right into her computer through the Wi-Fi and watch it whenever I want. It's delightful."

I hid a groan. "So, you and Margaret are cataloging everyone who comes and goes from that house?"

"Of course we are. One must find diversions where one can, dear. We have devised a ranking system for the visitors. Would you like to see?"

I opened my mouth to answer. The inn chimed, projecting an image of Thek. The First Scholar's headdress sat askew, and his feathers stuck out in all directions, fully erect and making him look twice his size. Outraged squawking, screeching, and thudding filled the room. Feathers flew over the blood-smeared floor. A koo-ko body hurtled through the air behind Thek with a piercing battle screech. Thek clutched his head-dress and ducked, screaming over the clamor, "I require assistance!"

I waved an apology at Caldenia and took off running.

———

IT WAS AMAZING HOW FAST AN INNKEEPER COULD MOVE THROUGH the inn when properly motivated. It took me three seconds to land in the middle of the koo-ko fray and half a second to snap my fingers. Holes burst in the ceiling, releasing five-foot-tall metal claws on flexible metal tails. Each of the claws had six prongs coated in a thick layer of a rubber-like polymer, rendering them smooth and slightly springy. The claws dove into the melee, snapping up the koo-ko. Once the targets were caught, the claw's prongs locked, forming a cage around the koo-ko and retracting back to the ceiling. The philosophers ran, but my claws were faster.

The final koo-ko dashed toward the left channel in a desperate attempt to glide away, but the last claw swept under him, neatly scooping him up.

The First Scholar stared at the row of cages suspended just below the ceiling. "Well. I have never seen this arrangement before. Very effective."

"Thank you."

Most of the combatants had given up, but a few koo-ko still hurled themselves against the bars of their cages, still overcome by battle madness. I had designed the bars very carefully. They flexed outward with each blow, preventing the koo-ko from injuring themselves.

"The last inn I visited flooded the chamber with glue," Thek confessed.

"I'm familiar with that method, but the last time it was used, one of the guests panicked and bit through his own leg with his beak trying to escape."

"I have heard of this. Indeed, your method is far superior."

The koo-ko were small and plump but very agile, and when agitated, they darted around like a wide receiver with a football in his hands. The innkeepers had attempted to solve the problem of restraining them for centuries. Everything from a pulse of blinding light to knockout gas had been tried. Unfortunately, the light had caused partial blindness, knockout gas resulted in at least one fatality, and trapping them in their own tiny chambers caused deep psychological damage. Koo-kos lived in flocks. Separating them from each other led to an immediate and acute spike of anxiety, especially if light and sound deprivation methods were utilized. The cages were my answer. They could still see each other, they could scream at each other, their movement wasn't restrained, but they couldn't hurt themselves or each other.

The center of each cage's ceiling lit up, scanning the beings within. A thin stalk sprouted from the floor in front of me and bloomed into a screen. I scrolled through the scan's results. "Two broken bones, three dislocated wings, and a dozen minor lacerations. My congratulations, First Scholar. No fatalities and no eyes were lost."

"That's a relief." Thek sighed.

The inn's floor bristled with nozzles. A disinfecting mist erupted over the amphitheater, washing blood and smears of feces off the floor, seats, and the podium.

"If I may ask, what is the purpose of the small tiger?" Thek asked.

I turned around. Olasard, otherwise known as the Ripper of Souls, sat by the door.

"What are you doing here?"

The large Maine Coon cat looked at me with his big green eyes. I had rescued him from a glass box in the nearby PetSmart about a year ago. Now he moved through the inn as he pleased, and for some mysterious reason, Gertrude Hunt accommodated his wanderings.

"He's a pet," I explained.

Olasard chose that moment to walk over and rub on my legs. I picked him up and he sprawled in my arms, purring up a storm. I kept a good hold on him. Thek was on the larger side as far as koo-ko went, technically too large to be considered house cat prey, but it never hurt to be careful.

"Is the debate over for today?" I asked.

Thek surveyed the dangling cages. "Regrettably, a period of meditation is in order."

I waved my hand. The cages slid to opposite sides of the chamber. The bridges retracted, and the claws released their captives, who glided to the floor by their respective coops. The philosophers stumbled about, trying to regain some measure of dignity. Two automated medical chambers slid out of the floor, looking like six-foot-tall glossy metal spheres. The spheres slid open and the first of the injured combatants ambled over to them.

"All is well that ends well," the First Scholar declared.

Magic tugged on me. Someone had parked by the inn.

"In that case, please excuse me," I said. "I'm needed elsewhere."

"Thank you for your timely assistance," Thek said.

I nodded, walked out into the hallway, and set Olasard on the floor. "Stay away from the koo-ko."

Olasard purred.

"I'm serious. They will kill you, and it's not a euphemism."

Olasard stretched. Why I was having this conversation with a cat was beyond me.

Beast tore down the corridor toward me, exploding into barks. She must have gone outside through the doggy door and she didn't like what she'd found out there.

"Front camera feed."

I marched down the hallway. The feed from the inn's front cameras slid on the wall in front of me, trying to keep up. On it, a fit man in a black suit got out of the back seat of a black SUV, looked around, and opened the front passenger door. An older man wearing an expensive trench coat and sunglasses got out and stared at Gertrude Hunt.

For some reason, Sean's description of him made me expect a good ole boy or a version of a human buzzard with a bald head and beady eyes. This man wasn't that. Tall, trim, he would have been at home on the streets of London or New York. His skin was a golden bronze, the kind fashion magazines photoshop onto the models when they want to convey health, wealth, and vacations in tropical places. His features were universally handsome: defined, dimpled chin, a square jaw, a wide mouth, a strong nose, carved cheek bones, and a broad forehead. His thick wavy hair, once dark and now salted with distinguished silver, was on the longer side of a short male haircut, shorter on his temples, and long enough to style on top.

He could have been from the Mediterranean, the Middle East, or Latin America, or he could have been an Englishman with a serious tan. Without seeing his eyes, it was hard to tell.

The man started up my driveway, his bodyguard shadowing him. They didn't pull up onto the property. Interesting.

I reached the front room, shrugged off my robe, and hung it

on the side hook. Beast let out a slow deep rumble by my feet. I picked her up, just in case.

The pair approached the front door. The older man looked for a bell, didn't find one, and settled for knocking on the screen door. I let him knock for a few seconds and answered.

"Good afternoon. Can I help you?"

The older man took off his sunglasses. His eyes were solid black and piercing, like two chunks of shiny coal set into his face.

"Is she here?" His voice was deep and powerful, and he sounded like a man used to issuing commands.

I could play dumb, or I could acknowledge the meeting. Playing dumb seemed pointless, since I would have to let him in at the appointed time.

"You are too early, Mr. Peterson," I told him.

He looked over my shoulder at the front room. "I want a room."

"We have no vacancy. There are two hotels down the street within two miles of here."

"I'll pay you a thousand dollars per night."

"No, you won't. We have no vacancy."

"Ten thousand dollars per night."

"Mr. Peterson, there are rules to this meeting. You must abide by them or it won't take place."

His eyebrows came together. He jerked his head at his bodyguard. The other man moved toward the door. They were planning to force their way in. Either they had discussed this en route or bullying his way into people's houses was a normal thing for Rudolph Peterson.

There were a million ways I could stop them, most of which would betray the special nature of the inn to two humans. I settled on the simplest.

The bodyguard grasped the door handle of the screen door

and pulled. The door remained shut. I had fused it into the wall. From the outside, it looked normal, but from the inside, the hinges and the outline of the door disappeared, melting into the wall.

The bodyguard stopped pulling and pushed. The door remained shut.

Peterson looked at him. The bodyguard locked his teeth, grasped the door handle, planted his foot against the wall, and pulled. He was remarkably strong, but he was trying to pull down the entire front wall.

The bodyguard let go, spun a kick, and hammered his heel into the door. It didn't even shudder.

Peterson grimaced. "Cut it."

The bodyguard pulled out a folding knife, flicked it open with a practiced twist of his wrist, and slashed at the screen. The knife glanced off with a spray of sparks. My screens were made from an advanced metal alloy. It would repel prolonged fire from a squad level assault weapon at point blank range.

The bodyguard looked at Peterson.

I petted Beast.

The short *whoop* of a police siren turned on for two seconds and echoed down the street. A black-and-white cruiser pulled up behind the SUV. Officer Marais got out, made a show of checking the SUV's license plate, and marched up to my front door. Sean must have gotten ahold of him after all.

Peterson gave Marais a tough stare. Marais looked back at him with that flat cop expression that made you feel guilty even if you hadn't done anything, because that look said you must have done something and now there would be consequences.

Marais finished looking at Peterson and decided to look at the bodyguard instead. His stare slid to the knife in the bodyguard's hand.

The bodyguard looked uncomfortable.

Marais put his hand on his service weapon. "Drop the knife."

The bodyguard let go of the blade and it fell to the porch.

"I have received a report of trespassing at this address. Ma'am, would you like these two men to leave?"

"I would."

Marais pivoted to Peterson. "Sir, please exit the property."

Peterson threw me a sharp look, his black eyes unreadable, turned and walked down the driveway without a word. The bodyguard followed. Marais winked at me, slid the cop expression back on, and trailed Peterson and his bodyguard down the driveway.

On one hand, knowing Sean worried about me and Marais cared enough to protect me made me warm and fuzzy. On the other hand, when Sean came back, I would have to go over the innkeeper policy with regard to exposure and seeking outside assistance. Plus, I totally had this. At no point were Peterson and his bodyguard coming into our inn, and the hardest thing about this whole ordeal had been making sure Beast didn't show them her real teeth.

Marais aside, mission accomplished. Peterson hadn't entered the inn and nothing out of the ordinary happened to make him suspect that Gertrude Hunt was anything other than a typical bed and breakfast. With a remarkably strong screen door.

On the street, the bodyguard opened the front passenger door for Peterson. The Evil Millionaire moved to get in, turned his head, and froze.

A very large man walked up to the inn. He wore a full-length leather coat and cowboy boots and he was making an odd metallic jangle as he walked. His hair was long and fell to his shoulders in perfectly symmetrical golden blond waves, as if he had spent a staggering amount of time with a curling iron and then killed half of the planet's ozone layer spraying it in place. His features reminded me of someone from Polynesia, a Māori or a Hawaiian, but something was definitely off about the proportions.

And who might you be?

The bodyguard gaped at the giant, his mouth slightly slack. Peterson squinted, as if aiming a gun. Both he and the bodyguard were a couple of inches above six feet, and this man towered a full foot or more above them.

I pulled up a screen and zoomed in on his face. The man's irises were a brilliant, vivid magenta, the exact color of a spinel ring Caldenia pondered buying last year and dismissed as "too pink."

The stranger fluttered his unnaturally long blond eyelashes and opened his mouth.

Don't speak, don't speak, don't speak...

"Greetings, local keeper of the peace."

I groaned.

"Can I help you, sir?" Marais asked, the same flat expression on his face.

"Might I inquire about the location of the closest lodging house?"

Marais didn't bat an eye. "Up that driveway." He nodded to indicate Gertrude Hunt.

"I thank you muchly," the stranger declared. "Fare thee well, constable."

He turned and jangled up my driveway. I zoomed in on his feet. His boots had spurs.

Who had I upset in my previous life?

The man raised his shovel sized hands and held them together, touching his index and middle fingers at the top and his thumbs at the bottom, forming a diamond space between. A Medamoth with a humanizer. Just what we needed.

I raised my hands, interlacing my fingers and holding them straight with thumbs pressed against palms, so my hands formed an x.

"Greetings, innkeeper."

"Welcome, honored guest."

He grasped the door handle, the screen door swung open effortlessly, and he ducked inside.

I glimpsed Peterson as I shut the door. He stared at me, jaw bulging and face as pale as a corpse.

I shut the door. Five minutes. If only the Medamoth had shown up five minutes later.

I turned around, retrieved my robe and slipped it on.

The Medamoth stretched. His human body turned static, frozen, as if it were an image on pause, split into hexagons, which turned white, then rained down, as the projection collapsed, leaving a massive being in their wake. He stood eight feet tall, with broad shoulders and powerfully muscled limbs. His skin, deep green on his back, and bright orange on his front, looked thick and rough, like the hide of some prehistoric shark. His legs had more in common with a kangaroo than with a human, but his arms were fully humanoid, long, with large hands equipped with four dexterous digits, each tipped with a claw. His head belonged to a predator—long terrifying jaws, designed to pierce struggling prey with four inch fangs and hold it still as it thrashed, dying; large canine ears, standing straight; a sensitive nose at the end of a long muzzle; and large amber eyes, front set, like the eyes of Earth's predators, to notice and track prey.

The Medamoths were born hunters. Tracking, hunting, and killing was instinctual to them, and their predatory drive kicked in as soon as they opened their eyes. A baby Medamoth released into a meadow would kill every rabbit and mouse in it, gorge themselves, and then cry because the rest of the meat rotted and now they were hungry. The Assembly classified them as high risk. There had been cases of them trying to hunt other guests, and some busier inns, like Casa Feliz, were reluctant to take them, because they had to be closely supervised.

I had an inn full of delicious plump koo-ko and a Drífan liege lord was coming.

The Medamoth wore a voluminous robe of undyed plant-based fabric, reminiscent of linen. Normally they wore an assortment of weapons and metal jewelry studded with gemstones. He wore a knotted rope around his neck, decorated with plain wooden beads. An identical rope hugged his waist. A red tattoo marked the back of his neck, standing out against the green and luminescing slightly, so the troops behind him could see his rank during a battle and know who to follow.

"That's better," he said.

I spun a hallway off the left side of the front room and motioned for him to enter. "Please join me, General Who Sinks His Fangs Into The Throat Of His Enemy."

He shook his hand at me in a dismissive gesture. "No rank please. Today I'm just a pilgrim."

We strolled through the hallway. I had built arched windows into it on the fly, and the sunshine flooded through, drawing golden patterns on the wood floor.

"What brings you to Earth?"

"I'm being groomed for a government position."

"Congratulations."

He grimaced, baring nightmarish fangs. "While many may view it as a prestigious position, it's simply another way to serve. I have served, I will serve."

"May I inquire as to the nature of the position?"

"Colonial governor. It's a frontier position. Conflict is expected."

"Why?"

"Because the colony is in a contested system. The other planet is occupied."

"By whom?"

"The Hope-Crushing Horde."

That explained volumes. "The Horde exists to acquire new territory. "

He showed his teeth again. "So my predecessor found out. Our settlement is well defended, we breed faster than the Otrokar, and the logistics are on our side. However, the Horde does not know the meaning of reason. We are hunters. We have learned to adapt to the limits of our biosphere. The Horde is a swarm that devours all and moves on."

Strictly speaking, the Horde did not devour. By ancient custom, each Otrokar who joined the Horde was entitled to a homestead. The homestead, in Otrokar terms, meant a parcel of land about fifteen acres, large enough to grow some food and pasture their mounts. The higher your rank, the bigger the homestead. Despite the modern convenience of cities, almost all Horde veterans claimed the homestead at the end of their service. They had to expand.

"To become worthy of the office," the Medamoth continued, "one must complete a pilgrimage with the purpose of learning a valuable understanding."

"An interesting custom. I can think of several Earth politicians in need of such a pilgrimage."

"It does change your perspective."

"What understanding do you seek?"

The general's eyes narrowed. "I'm visiting the sites of great last stands, where a small group of defenders fought against overwhelming odds."

"Are you learning how to die well, general?"

He made a low coughing noise, the Medamoth version of a laugh. "I'm learning what went wrong. What led to that last desperate defense? Why didn't they surrender? Why didn't the larger force employ diplomacy to prevent the slaughter? I have visited Nexus, Urdukor, Daesyn, and now I come to Earth. It's the final leg of my pilgrimage."

Urdukor belonged to the Hope-Crushing Horde, Daesyn was the planet of House Krahr, and the Nexus was the battleground where the Otrokar and the vampires of the Holy Anocracy butchered each other for decades until they reached a peace treaty in Gertrude Hunt. He wasn't on a pilgrimage of last stands. He was trying to figure out how to not die in one.

Coming to this inn was no coincidence. He wanted to know the secret to making peace with the Horde.

"I know that my kind isn't always welcome at the inns of Earth."

It was my turn to show teeth. "Your species tries to eat the other guests."

The general looked abashed. "My pilgrimage is vital. I give you my word of honor that I will restrain my hunting impulses. I wish to request a room at your inn. I understand that Treaty Stay requires you to accept my presence, but I don't wish to impose against your will. I will require some assistance in viewing my chosen last stand, so I humbly ask for your acceptance."

"Which site are you here to view?"

"The Alamo."

Of all the last stands on Earth, he picked the Alamo. It couldn't be Masada, Stalingrad, Thermopylae, or Shiroyama. It had to be the Alamo. Technically we were the closest inn, but he could have gone to Casa Feliz as well. He was here because we had done the impossible and he wanted to know how we had done it.

"Gertrude Hunt is honored to welcome you as a guest. I have to warn you, we are expecting a Drífan."

His ears flicked up. "I do not anticipate a conflict," he said carefully.

"Then let me show you to your rooms. One last thing, your disguise needs a little work."

"The humanizer? I thought I had done rather well calibrating it. I chose attractive male features, the popular hair color, and the jewel eyes the experts say humans prize."

He thought he'd made himself pretty.

"Was I not successful?"

"Not entirely."

"Was I too frightening?"

"More like disconcerting."

The Medamoth coughed again. I twisted the hallway, turning it into a staircase, and opened an oversized door at its end. A round chamber of pale stone lay ahead, with curved couches supporting plush blue cushions along the walls. Weapons decorated the room, displayed on the walls between the jewel-colored replicas of Medamoth tapestries. A large screen offered a plethora of Earth channels, playing a preview of a National Geographic special on Alaska. A dipping pool waited to one side, sunken into the floor next to the balcony, which offered a view of the orchard and the evening sky above. It was almost dinner time.

"Have you eaten?"

"I have. I will spend the evening adjusting to the time change and resting in contemplation. Please call me Qoros. It's the name I have chosen for this journey."

"Please call me Dina. If you need anything, simply ask the inn or call me by name."

I left and shut the door behind me. We had until midnight. In every known account of the Drífen visiting, they always arrived just a couple of minutes before the clock struck twelve. That left Orro with roughly seven hours to come up with the Grand Burger, and I hadn't heard him yell "fire!" since the tea with Caldenia.

I had a feeling that something had gone terribly wrong.

[5]

I sat at the kitchen table, facing Caldenia. Two glasses of water and two plates waited between us. The first plate contained a freshly purchased Grand Burger. The second held its exact replica. It looked like the real thing—plump sesame-seed bun, thin patty, a stack of lettuce, pickles, and tomato, and melted yellow cheese. It smelled like the real thing.

We had now bought thirty Grand Burgers, which had caused no end of fun making by the Favor delivery driver. Red Deer wasn't that large, so we had gotten the same delivery driver three times in a row for an identical order of ten burgers each. When she made the final delivery, she asked if the Hamburglar was renting a room or if we were just making a documentary about fast food.

To the right, Orro stood completely still in the kitchen, like a monument to culinary failure.

Caldenia and I regarded each other like two duelists. Both burgers had been cut in half with surgical precision.

"Shall we?" Caldenia inquired.

I picked up my half of the Grand Burger and took a bite. It

tasted just like the other four Grand Burgers I had tasted in the last four hours. I swallowed, drank some water, and picked up Orro's burger. The first burger he presented to us several hours earlier tasted like heaven. The second was too chewy, the third was too mushy, the fourth was too salty. Taking another bite was kind of scary.

I inhaled and bit into the burger.

Cardboard. Soaked in meat juice.

Caldenia picked up a napkin and delicately spat into it. "You know I live for your cooking, dear, but this wasn't one of your better efforts."

Orro moved. Claws fanned my face and the two plates vanished, their contents hurled into the garbage. Orro leaned against the island, his back to the countertop, his face raised to the heavens, his arms hanging limp by his sides.

"I cannot do it."

The defeat in his voice was so absolute, I wanted to hug him.

"Of course you can't," Caldenia said. "You simply cannot make bad food."

"I should be able to replicate it. It's a simple dish. I have all the ingredients." He sounded so hollow.

"This hamburger is not natural," I told him. "Most dishes evolve naturally. Stews have meat and root vegetables because livestock is slaughtered in early winter and root vegetables keep well in the cellar through the cold months. Spring salad is called that because it's made with the leafy greens and grasses available in early spring. The hamburger is an artificial construct. Cows are slaughtered in winter, tomatoes are best in late summer, lettuce is in season in spring, and that's not counting the extra cow required to produce the milk used to make cheese for the patty and butter for the bun."

Orro stared at me.

"It's mass-produced, inexpensive, and meant to be quick and convenient, but still pack enough calories to be filling." I couldn't tell if I was making any headway. "They use a particular cut of meat for it, likely the cheapest possible, and they add things to it, which accounts for the texture and moisture of the patty. No matter what I do to ground beef, it doesn't have that texture."

"But you don't have my training and experience. I have tried everything," Orro said, his voice still flat. "I added fat, I added stock, I emulsified the meat. I have tried corn starch, oils, and spices. For the sake of this hamburger, I have committed the sin of adding MSG and silicone dioxide. It's all for naught. I'm a failure."

He spun around and marched out of the kitchen.

I took a deep breath and slowly blew the air out.

"We have to let him stew in his despair," Caldenia said. "Otherwise, we may never again be served a decent meal."

"That's a bit harsh, your Grace."

"Coddling never leads to improvement."

The inn's magic brushed against me, as if someone had tossed a rock into a placid pond and the waves from it splashed against me. Someone had crossed the inn's boundary.

It was past nine, and Sean was still out.

I called up a screen from the northeast side of the property. Four people in dark clothes crept through the brush. They wore black balaclavas that hid their heads and faces except for a narrow strip around the eyes and carried submachine guns.

I pivoted the screen to Caldenia with a flick of my fingers. "Rudolph Peterson's ninjas."

Caldenia rubbed her hands together. "Would it be too presumptuous to ask for one? I've been eating these dreadful hamburgers."

"You know our policy. Gertrude Hunt doesn't serve sentient beings as food."

Caldenia rolled her eyes.

The four "commandos" snuck through the bushes, painstakingly careful where they put their feet. The original plan was to pretend to be just a normal establishment, but guns upped the stakes.

If Sean were home, he would hunt them down, put their heads on a pike, and then present it to Peterson like a shish kebab.

I tapped my fingers on the table. The leading ninja, a man, judging by the height and the shoulders, sank into the ground up to his knees.

Everyone froze.

The intruders scanned the brush, listening for any noises. When nothing out the ordinary happened, two of them stepped closer to their leader and tried to pull him out. I let them work him free and then sank the one on the left up to his hips.

Everyone froze again.

It took them three minutes to get their friend out. They huddled up and made fancy hand gestures, some of which included forceful pointing, making fists, and drawing lines across their throats. Finally, a consensus must have been reached, because they backed up a few yards, fanned out, and started north, trying to skirt the troublesome patch of ground.

I let them take ten steps and then sank the one on the right down to their knees.

Caldenia cracked a smile.

They pulled my victim out and formed a single line, the leader taking point. He unsheathed a large knife, hacked off a sapling, and tested the ground with it. The ground held. He raised his hand and moved two fingers, motioning the team forward. They started moving again, single file, each intruder putting his feet in the steps of the one in front of them.

I let them take fifteen steps and sank the last ninja into the ground down to their waist. The masked human frantically pawed the ground, as the team kept moving.

"Help," the ninja hissed in a female voice.

The leader whirled around. The balaclava hid his face, but his body radiated "what the fuck" with every cell of his being. The two other gate-crashers grabbed their sunken friend and tried to pull her out. I held her still.

They strained.

One, two, three…

The intruder popped free with sudden force and the three ninjas collapsed on the ground in a heap. Caldenia chuckled.

The leader raised his arms.

The three ninjas scrambled upright. The woman I had sunk dusted off her pants, pointed to herself, and jabbed her thumb to the right, indicating the direction they had come from.

The leader shook his head and pointed toward the inn.

The female ninja shook her head.

The leader pointed to himself, pointed to the ninja, and pointed at the inn again.

The female ninja gave him the finger, pretended to wash her hands off, and raised them in the air.

I sank the three remaining ninjas down to their armpits.

The woman nodded, executed a crisp about-face, and marched back the way they had come.

"The voice of reason," Caldenia commented. "She deserves the chance to skulk another day."

I raised my eyebrows. "Mercy, your Grace?"

"Natural selection," Caldenia said.

The door to Baha-char opened deep within the inn. Sean.

In thirty seconds, he came into the kitchen, put his arms around me, and kissed me. He came back. The relief was so real, I almost slumped down in my seat.

63

Sean smiled at me and saw the screen. "Visitors?"

"Rudolph Peterson came to see us this afternoon."

"Do me a favor, hold them just like that."

Sean pulled off his shirt and walked out of the kitchen door.

On the screen, the three figures struggled to free themselves. Digging yourself out when you are in dirt up to your armpits was difficult under normal circumstances, and I had no intention of letting them go.

I felt Sean move through the grounds, unnaturally fast, and whispered, sending my voice to his ear. "Don't kill them."

The moon slipped out from behind a ragged grey cloud, flooding the scene with silver light. The brush parted.

The three struggling humans held still.

A lupine beast emerged from the undergrowth, so large, his head would be even with my chest. Sheathed in dark fur, huge, silent, the king of wolves lowered his head, his amber eyes glowing with reflected fire, and padded toward the three intruders.

They didn't move. They didn't blink or breathe, as his hand-sized paws landed next to them.

Sean circled them, inhaling their scent. He stopped before the leader, in plain view of the two others.

A long moment stretched by.

Sean opened his jaws. In the light of the moon, his fangs glinted like daggers. He bit the leader's head.

The ninja on the left screamed, a hoarse cry of pure fear.

"Oh dear," Caldania said. "I think he broke that one."

Sean pulled the man's mask off and spat it to the side. The leader gaped at him, a light-skinned man in his early forties, with brown hair cut military short, his eyes glassy and wide open.

Sean lowered his head and stared at the man, his fangs an inch from the intruder's face. For a torturous few seconds nobody moved. Then Sean turned and melted back into the darkness of the woods.

I jettisoned the ninjas from the dirt. They scrambled to their feet and ran back the way they came.

———

Sean had bought enough spare parts and weapons to outfit a small army, so much so, that he could only carry a small fraction of his purchases, which he referred to as the "really cool stuff."

"A three-coil liquefier?"

Sean hefted the six-foot-long cannon that resembled some ridiculous video game gun. Two tendrils of striated wood slithered from the ceiling, wrapped around the gun, and sucked it up. Gertrude Hunt and he seemed to have no trouble communicating.

"Why would you ever feel the need to turn carbon-based life-forms into primordial soup?"

"Because it's easier to dispose of the remains."

"Why not an anti-matter death ray then?" I was only half joking. There were several weapons in existence that would have qualified for that description.

He winked at me. "Liquefier was on sale."

I rubbed my face, trying to adjust to the new arsenal. Above us, Gertrude Hunt creaked, installing the cannon.

I've had to shut down the koo-ko "discussions" twice in the past four hours. A liquefier was entirely too much temptation at the moment.

"Wilmos is going to deliver the rest tomorrow. Do you think we have enough firepower to survive one night with the Drífen in the house?"

"Oh, I don't know," I loaded a house's worth of sarcasm into my voice. "We will have to muddle through somehow."

"I said I was sorry about Marais."

"I appreciate the two of you conspiring to keep me safe, but the inn and I had it under control and there are strict rules that govern what we can and cannot do. Marais is not a guest. He's not staff. He's an aware outsider. That means that the responsibility for his awareness and what he might do with it rests on our shoulders. You already broke the rules when you gave him a subatomic vaporizer. If the Assembly finds out, it will create a problem."

Sean grunted. "First, Marais is cool. Second, the vaporizer is telepathically linked to him and is indistinguishable from a normal police baton. It's harmless, until he decides it's not. Third, I keep hearing how the Assembly doesn't like this and there will be trouble if they find out about that. What has this Assembly ever done for you?"

"They gave me a magic inn and access to a treasure trove of galactic knowledge."

"They gave you an inn that was a hair away from dying, and you nursed it back to health, while they didn't lift a finger to help."

I held out my hand. Sean's copper robe fell out of the ceiling into my fingers. I thrust it at him. "It's fifteen minutes till midnight. Put the robe on and quit complaining. You knew the deal when you signed up."

"You sound like my drill sergeants."

I stuck my tongue out at him and we went down to the kitchen, as he slipped on his robe.

The backyard had been transformed. Colorful lanterns hung in the air, lavender, pink, green, and a warm, happy yellow. Lengths of silky fabric draped the outer wall of the inn, curving to both sides, forming canopies over the porch and part of the lawn. Delicate lantern flowers, turquoise, pink, and magenta, bloomed on the lawn. To the left, a pair of lantern peacocks the size of a car, perched among the flowers. To the right, a lantern tiger pair guarded their cub. A path stretched from the porch to the spot where the Drífan herald had entered yesterday, bordered by lantern jellyfish, suspended from nearly invisible wires. Their colorful paper tentacles swayed in the breeze.

It was just me and Sean. Caldenia was watching from her quarters, but I didn't think it would be wise for her to be present. Orro had disappeared into his rooms. When I had notified him that the Drífen were incoming, he hadn't responded.

The night was quiet. A cold wind stirred my hair.

Sean reached into his sleeve and pulled out a flower. It was white and frilly, with brilliant blue specks on the petals and a deep blue center. He held it out to me.

Awww. He brought me a flower.

I took it and smelled it. "Thank you. It's lovely."

We were standing on the porch together at midnight, with the magical lanterns glowing all around us. In a few moments, all hell could break loose, but for now it was just us. When I got old, I would remember this moment, the moment when Sean brought me a flower from Baha-char.

The Drífen arrived.

There was no power surge, no bright light from the sky, no gate in the fabric of existence. They simply appeared at the edge of the field and walked toward us. There were six of them: Zedas; the Akeraat from the previous evening; the small creature that had accompanied him; a very large woman in silver armor, with nearly white skin and equally pale hair, carrying a halberd on her back, a man dressed in black with dark brown skin and a wealth of glossy dark hair pulled back from his face, who was like a dagger, compact, fast, and probably deadly; an olive skinned woman in her early forties, her hair twisted into elabo-rate knots, walking primly in a green and white robe; and in front of them all, a woman in her early thirties, wrapped in an old cloak.

I searched for their magic. The woman in the cloak felt almost inert, but the others were saturated with power. I could feel them moving through the inn grounds, dense concentrated knots of magic. Gertrude Hunt creaked.

Steady. I won't let them hurt you.

They came within fifteen feet of us and stopped.

"Greetings, innkeepers," the woman in the cloak said. "Thank you for accepting my request and extending your hospitality to us."

This was the liege lord? I didn't know who I expected but she wasn't it. She looked perfectly normal. About thirty, maybe thirty-five, with deep bronze skin, pretty, athletic build, average height. The only remarkable thing about her were her dark eyes, the same nearly black as Rudolph Peterson's, and dark green hair. Even here in Red Deer, Texas, I saw people with green hair on a regular basis. I could have passed her in the store and never looked twice.

My brain was still processing, but my mouth was already moving. "Welcome, honored guests. Let me show you to your rooms."

The door behind me slid to the side. A hallway formed, cutting straight through the kitchen and other rooms, sectioned off from them with invisible walls. I didn't want any interference.

The liege lord and I entered, walking side by side. Behind us, her entourage followed. Sean brought up the rear and the tunnel collapsed behind him as soon as he passed.

"Did you make the call?" she asked. She seemed, not tired exactly, but resigned, like a person facing a mountain she didn't want to climb.

"I did. I told him your conditions. He arrived this morning."

"Did he try to force his way into your inn?"

"Twice. He did attempt to buy me first."

She glanced at me. There was a magnetic authority in her gaze. I still felt no magic.

"He cannot enter while I'm here," the liege lord said. "Not until the appointed time. I don't wish to see him."

"He won't be a problem," I told her.

"My uncle is the very definition of a problem. He's persistent."

That cinched it. She was definitely American. "Here I own the air we breathe. Your uncle won't enter without my permission."

"I hope so, innkeeper."

I had miscalculated with the bedroom. There was a weariness in her, a kind of bitter determination. She needed comfort in the worst way, and when we sought comfort, we went home. That's why the hamburger. She didn't want the beautiful Drífan bedroom. She wanted an echo of home.

I reached out with my magic, carving a new room off the bedroom I had made yesterday. And now the symmetry of the original bedroom was off. I frantically shifted the columns.

"Is something the matter, innkeeper?" the liege lord asked.

"No. Are you hungry?"

"Not tonight."

We came to the massive double doors. They swung open before us and the common room of the Drífan palace glittered beyond. The trick to building successful rooms wasn't in duplicating the guest's original environment. When they travelled, they wanted to see something new. If they arrived at an exact replica of the palace they left, they would be disappointed. Instead, a successful innkeeper took the elements of the original and used their imagination to create something new, familiar enough to be comfortable yet different enough to not feel stale.

The room in front of us kept the Drífan grandeur. The floor

was soft beige stone with marble swirls of paler white and flecks of gold. The walls were the color of ivory, the stone weathered, as if the palace was hundreds of years old. Two rows of columns, their bodies matching the walls, their tops elaborately decorated with bands of red agate and green malachite, supported a thirty-foot ceiling with a huge domed skylight in the center.

Straight ahead, my version of a stone throne, elaborately carved from purpleheart wood, beckoned with soft green cushions. Directly behind the throne a tapestry hung on the wall, a perfect replica of the view from the Drífan balcony, complete with the blue bird. I had Gertrude Hunt weave it from colorful synthetic silk. On both sides of the tapestry double doors offered access to a balcony. More doors, six specifically, branched off from both sides of the room, leading to individual bedrooms.

I had echoed the glowing purple of the throne and the green of malachite and the red of the agate through the room with accessories, decorative swords, alien vases, padded chairs, and side tables. Alien flowers and Earth shrubs bloomed in the corners from simple clay pots that could have been made at the start of time. It was a cohesive space, still ornate, still old, but serene and calming.

Zedas took a step forward, bowing slightly at the liege lord's right. "Is it suitable?"

"It is." The woman strode into the room.

"Your bedroom is the closest to the throne on the right," I specified. "My name is Dina. If you require anything, call me and the inn will notify me."

The Drífen walked into the room past me. The large woman grasped the double doors and shut them.

I was halfway down the stairs, when I heard a voice whisper in my ear, delivered by the inn's magic.

"Thank you for the room, Dina."

[6]

The morning of the first day of Treaty Stay started with breaking up another koo-ko debate. They had convened for an early morning ritual, which progressed into a spirited discussion, which then predictably degenerated into a brawl. This time nine of the combatants had needed the regeneration chamber. At the rate they were going, we'd have a fatality before the holiday was over. I had lost only one guest in the inn, and I'd made a promise to myself to never lose another.

The day had just started, and it looked like it was only going to get worse.

"When you told me we had a new guest, you neglected to mention he was a Medamoth." Sean loomed over me as I drank my first cup of tea.

In the depths of the kitchen, Orro moved like a dark wraith. He hadn't made a sound since storming off yesterday.

"I have him contained in his own wing. He's on a pilgrimage."

"A pilgrimage or an assassination attempt?"

"A pilgrimage. He's too high ranking to be an assassin. He's scheduled to assume the post of a colonial governor and the

71

Hope-Crushing Horde will be his new neighbors. He knows we brokered a peace on Nexus, and he designed this entire pilgrimage around our inn. He's trying to figure out how to make peace with the Otrokars."

Sean crossed his arms on his chest. "I had several Medamoths under my command on Nexus. They don't make peace. They kill, they hunt, and they write bad poetry."

I couldn't resist. Auul, the planet Sean's ancestors blew up rather than surrender to their enemies, was known as the planet of warrior poets. "So they are a poor imitation of a werewolf?"

"They are eight feet tall, homicidal, and rabid. They chase anything that moves and bite things without thinking."

I squinted at him. "What kind of bad poetry do they write?"

Sean gave me a look and recited, "Hunt. Hunt. The scent of prey. The light of the moon. Blood on the fang. Taste the heart-beat. Rapture."

I clapped. "That was lovely."

"What will be lovely is when he finds out about the space chickens. There will be a massacre. And guess what? The Assembly won't be happy about that."

I sipped more tea. "The koo-ko are fine," I lied.

"The Medamoths have an overwhelming prey drive. If it runs, they chase it." Sean looked up. "Show me the Medamoth rooms."

The inn produced a screen. On it Qoros stretched, holding a pose in a Medamoth version of yoga. His eyes were closed. He stood perfectly still, his right leg bent at the knee, foot resting against the inside of his left thigh, his arms spread wide.

"His name is Qoros, by the way."

Sean squinted at the tattoo on Qoros' neck. "Qoros my ass. That's Ratharr the Vein Ripper. He led the offensive on Mrelnos, took the capital and crushed the planetary government while outnumbered three to one. He is one of the Medamoth Bloody Twelve, the best heroes of the species. If he's a pilgrim, I'm…"

"An innkeeper?"

"Fine."

"His brother is a mercenary who was stationed on Nexus." I sipped my tea. "It's funny how you think that I don't know the identities of our guests or how to use facial recognition software."

"Fair enough. I shouldn't have assumed that you didn't do your homework on this guy."

"Thank you for your apology."

"Have you seen them fight though? I mean, up close."

"No."

"Put a cockroach on that wall, please."

I sorted through my storage, plucked a cockroach from the insect tank, and teleported it onto the wall. Qoros stood completely still, his eyes still closed. Even his ears didn't twitch.

A second ticked by.

The cockroach moved half a millimeter.

Qoros sprang up seven feet in the air, snatched the roach off the wall, and crushed it with his claws.

Sean pointed to the screen.

"You did the same thing two nights ago because you saw a mosquito."

"That mosquito would have qualified as air support."

"Look, he's here to see the Alamo. We are bound to respect his wishes during the Treaty Stay. He has a humanizer, and the sooner we calibrate it and take him to San Antonio, the faster he will leave."

Amber rolled over Sean's irises. The wolf in his eyes left the dark forest and showed me his big teeth. "Not we, I. I'm going to take him to San Antonio, and you will stay as far away from him as possible."

I gave him a smile. "That's so sweet of you."

On the screen Qoros studied the crushed cockroach impaled on his claw and threw it into the garbage can.

I realized that Orro had stopped moving and now stared at the two of us.

"Yes?"

"What is this humanizer?" he asked.

"It's an illusion device," I told him. "Sometimes guests have business on Earth or have to travel between the inns. If their dimensions are not too different from the human dimension, you can use the device to disguise them. It's expensive and rare, and it works on some species, but not others, and nobody knows why."

Orro's quills stood on end. He rushed at us, frantic, and clasped my hands into his. "I know what the problem is. Cooking is a collaborative art. One cannot become a chef in a vacuum. One must observe and learn from other masters; one must taste dishes not of his own making. I have neglected this cornerstone of my art, first during my exile and then after coming here. Look!"

He spun around and flicked his fingers. The TV screen on the wall came to life, showing a website with dates and times. The header on the website announced in big fiery letters "Garry Keys Fire and Lightning Show."

"The master, he'll be filming his show in San Antonio today. If only I could watch him work, I could break through the walls of the dungeon constraining me. I could adapt and overcome."

Oh no. Where had he even heard that?

"Garry Keys," Sean answered my unspoken question. "He started as an Army cook."

"Orro," I said gently. "The TV show is not like real life. It's staged. I don't think it would be like seeing him in the kitchen. I'm afraid you will be disappointed."

Orro struck a dramatic pose, pointing to the screen with a

clawed finger. "I have watched every minute of every show. There is nothing he can do to disappoint me."

I put my hands over my face.

"Please," Orro moaned.

"Is that even possible?" Sean asked me.

"Maybe. Most humanizers are area-of-effect devices. It would take a lot of calibration because of the difference in species. This is a horrible idea."

"Please, small human."

"I can talk to Qoros," Sean said.

"I can't believe you. You're proposing to take a Medamoth and a Quillonian on a field trip into a crowded human space. How are you going to keep them in line?"

Sean turned to Orro. "Do you think you can control yourself?"

Orro clamped his hand over the right side of his chest, which contained his layered heart. "I swear by the blood of my ancestors."

Sean pivoted back to me. "See? He's cool."

"What happens to Orro if the Vein Ripper goes nuts and his humanizer fails?"

"I'll be carrying the humanizer, and if Qoros steps out of line, I'll neutralize him and Orro will help me carry him to the car." Sean glanced at Orro. "Isn't that right, battle buddy?"

Orro rose to his full height, all quills erect, claws spread for the kill. "I will assist, combat friend."

"What makes you think Qoros will even agree to this?"

Sean flashed me a wolfish smile. "I can be very persuasive."

I set my tea down so hard my cup clinked. "You'd fight him. You'd beat up a guest to assert your dominance so he would respect you while you are taking him to Alamo."

"What?" Sean pretended to be shocked.

"Do whatever you want, Sean Evans, but I'm telling you now if you cause an incident and offend a guest during Treaty Stay, I'll be mad at you forever."

Sean seemed to consider it. "I can live with that. The real question is, what would the Assembly—"

I grabbed a kitchen towel and threw it at him. Sean caught it and laughed.

A voice floated to me, carried over by the inn. "Dina, could you bring me a cup of coffee with creamer, and could you do it without Zedas finding out?"

"Of course," I whispered in reply. I got up. "The liege lord wants a coffee. Sean, please don't mess this trip up. I know you're sick of me mentioning the Assembly, but if two aliens pop out of nowhere in the middle of the Alamo, they will take this inn away from us."

"I know." Sean hugged me to him. "Trust me."

———

I ROSE OUT OF THE FLOOR OF THE DRÍFAN'S PRIVATE ROOM carrying a tray with a French press filled with coffee, a mug, and a bottle of International Delight Sweet Cream. If the liege lord was disturbed by my sudden appearance, she didn't show it.

She sat in a padded chair facing the floor-to-ceiling window presenting us with a view of the orchard and the trees beyond. She didn't turn or acknowledge me, so I only saw the back of her head. Her green hair was twisted into a messy bun. I walked over to her, set the tray on the nearby coffee table, and pressed the lever of the French press.

Around us the room was quiet. I had gone for an early nineties feel to it. Wall-to-wall beige carpet, a bed with a flower bedspread, pastel lavender walls, oak furniture, matching desk and dresser: all of it was designed with maximum nostalgia in mind. If I'd calculated right, she would have been a teenager in the nineties.

Our most nostalgic memories formed when we were teenagers. You would think that early childhood memories would have the most impact, but no. For the majority of people, the teen years mattered most. The music, TV shows, books and friendships formed when we were teens held a special significance.

Teenage years brought puberty and a new need for freedom. For the first time in our lives, we made independent choices that clashed with the authority of our parents. We fought for the right to listen to our music, to wear our clothes, to dye our hair, to like other people, and to make decisions affecting our future. And for the first time we experienced real consequences based on our actions and learned that parents, even innkeeper parents, were not gods and some things couldn't be fixed.

When I thought back to my childhood, the kid version of me was an amorphous, fuzzy memory. The teenage me was the first me, a preview of who I would become as an adult. She had definite opinions, thought her parents were stupid, and she knew everything about everything, but she was unmistakably me.

I poured the coffee into the mug and turned to leave.

"Will you sit with me?" she asked. A slight Southern accent tinted her voice, but I couldn't place it.

"Of course." I summoned a second chair, identical to the first, moved the coffee table between them, and sat.

The Drífan wore plain pants and a simple tunic of soft pale-green fabric. Her bare feet were tucked in under her. She poured a ridiculously large amount of creamer into her mug, smelled it and sipped a little. "Mmm."

"Does Zedas not approve of coffee?" I asked.

"Zedas does not approve of a great many things. He claims coffee disrupts the inner energy."

"Does it?"

"No. Zedas wants me to forget what it's like to be human. He doesn't know this room exists and I plan to keep it that way."

I had guessed right. "Why is it important for you to forget?"

She looked out the window. If I had to pick just one word to describe her, it would be "mournful." A profound, deep sadness wrapped around her like a shroud. She seemed worn out, like an ornate sword that had seen too many battles. The repeated strikes had worn off the fancy script on its blade, leaving it stripped bare and even more deadly.

"He thinks that if I forget, I won't be tempted to return. He wants me to leave Adira Kline behind permanently."

"Can you return?"

"That's a complicated question." Adira sipped a little more of her coffee. "The Mountain chose me. It didn't ask. Twelve thousand souls depend on my leadership. Walking away would throw them into chaos. And even if I did, my life here was severed when I left. It's been six years. Not so long, but it feels like a lifetime. I don't know if I could fit back into the old me, into her life. Sometimes I try her on for size, and she's like an old jacket that I outgrew. It smells familiar, and it holds the right memories, but it's too constraining."

"I'm sorry," I told her, and meant it.

"Thank you. I never wanted adventure. I suppose I'm a hobbit by nature. I was perfectly happy with a mundane life and ticking items off my list: going to school, getting a job, buying a car, getting a mortgage…"

She fell silent.

"Do you miss it?"

"Yes." Pain sharpened her voice slightly. She caught herself. "It's a moot point anyway. I promised Zedas that if he agreed to this meeting, I would never again open a doorway to Earth. This is my goodbye."

"Forgive me if I'm wrong, but doesn't Zedas serve you?"

"Yes." Adira sighed. "Life in my world is treacherous. Prospective liege lords train for decades, learning how to survive imperial politics, discovering how to harness magic, studying strategy and tactics. There are nine ways to greet an official depending on their rank, and the wrong bow or the incorrect inflection can mean the difference between peaceful life and the extermination of your dryht."

It didn't sound like a fun place.

"When I started, I knew nothing. I barely had six months of instruction before the Emperor invited my adoptive father to his court. It wasn't an invitation one could refuse and my conduct in his absence would determine if he lived or died. Zedas held my hand through all of it. If it wasn't for his guidance, the Green Mountain would have been overrun. So yes, I could ignore Zedas, and if I issued an order, he would obey, even against his better judgment."

"But you won't?"

"I won't. Unless I have no choice."

I had no room to talk, not after signing off on Orro's San Antonio trip.

"Zedas isn't wrong," she said softly. "I can't live in two worlds at once. That's why I am here. To get rid of baggage I no longer need."

She fell silent. In a way we were polar opposites. She had travelled to a new place and it forever changed her, so much that she couldn't go back. I always tried to escape the world of my childhood, but after ping-ponging all over the galaxy, I had come back to do exactly what my parents did.

"I've been contemplating the meaning of mercy," Adira said. "Are you merciful, Dina?"

I only managed one cup of tea this morning. It wasn't enough for philosophical discussions. "Mercy implies power and sacrifice."

Adira raised her eyebrows.

"Mercy is defined as kindness or forgiveness given to someone who is within your power to punish. To show mercy means to give up retribution, sometimes at the cost of justice. My hands are often tied. The safety of my guests is my priority. If I face someone who attempted to harm those in my charge, I must consider the possibility that if I let them go, they may try to hurt my guests again. I cannot allow that. I can't afford to take that risk."

"Did you show mercy to my uncle's people when they tried to invade your inn?"

I frowned. "I suppose it can be seen as mercy. But most of it was prudence. Any sudden death or disappearance would be investigated. The inns must avoid attention."

"Only if he reported them missing. He wouldn't. My uncle has waited for this meeting since he was nineteen years old, before I was even born."

That made no sense. "Do you think he will resort to violence when you meet him?"

She smiled. "There will be violence, but he won't be the one initiating it."

Crap. "Do you plan to kill your uncle here, on the premises?"

"I haven't decided. We were talking about mercy. If you had a chance to show it, would you?"

The answer felt very important, and I wasn't sure why. "It would depend on the person. Are they worthy of mercy? If I let them go, would they do harm or good? Perhaps it's more about their character than mine. Or yours."

Adira laughed softly. "Is it really that easy? What if you had a choice; to kill or to spare?"

"Killing a sentient being comes at a great emotional cost to me. Even if I am completely justified in it, I feel guilt and regret. I try to avoid it whenever I can. But I have my duty and if my obligations dictate that I remove a threat, I must."

"Thank you for the company," Adira said, setting her cup onto the tray. "I enjoyed speaking with you."

On the way to the kitchen, I realized that Adira Kline, who was without equal, killed her enemies by the thousands, sheltered her friends, and was feared by warriors, respected by scholars, beloved by her dryht, and recognized by the Emperor, was deeply unhappy. She'd come to Earth for the last time and it broke her heart.

She was my guest and I had no idea how to help her.

[7]

I sat in a chair on the back porch, drinking iced tea and eating lemon muffins, and watched Sean dance around Qoros. The Medamoth attacked with vicious quickness, leaping and striking. Sean glided out of the way, as if he'd known where Qoros would land before he started.

The koo-ko had resumed their debate, and I was keeping an eye on them. The prospect of meeting his idol gave Orro a boost and he prepared a luxurious breakfast for everyone and then made me a batch of lemon muffins. I knew a bribe when I saw one, but I would be a fool to turn it down. Now Orro was marathoning his favorite 'Fire and Lightning' episodes in preparation. Caldenia immersed herself in the Laurents' divorce. Rudolph Peterson stationed a spy across the street in a silver Ford Fusion. The man had been there since before sunrise, and around nine I brought him coffee and one of Orro's lemon muffins. He seemed terribly embarrassed.

Adira and her people remained in their rooms. She hid her magic so well, I still wasn't sure she had any. But her people brimmed with power, floating on the edge of my senses. It was like the Drífen room was a jar filled with glowing fireflies. Normally I afforded the guests privacy, but they were a special case, and I watched them quietly.

Zedas spent most of his time drinking tea and playing a complex version of chess with the man in black. They must have brought the board with them, because I'd never seen it before. The big white woman alternated between sleeping and watching TV. The older woman spent a great deal of time laying out Adira's clothes and mending them. The little beast, who was a he, and whose name was Saro, had spent a large portion of the morning curled up, napping with his tail over his face, but in the last half hour had become restless. He dug through his bags, looked around the room, and tried to go out the door, but the big white woman told him no.

On the lawn, Qoros jumped up six feet in the air to deliver a devastating kick to Sean's temple. If it had landed, Sean's head would have been torn off his shoulders. "If" was the operative word. Sean leaned out of the way, let the kick whistle by him, grabbed Qoros' leg, and dumped him unceremoniously on the ground. The Medamoth rolled to his feet.

I didn't have Sean's combat experience, but even I saw a pattern. Most or all of Qoros' strikes were designed to take advantage of his claws and his superior size. He almost never punched, he raked and swiped. His kicks aimed to get his victim on the ground. Once he had his victim on the ground, he'd pin it down with his weight and rip out its throat. If sabretooth tigers had evolved to stand on two legs and then developed sentience, they would fight just like that.

Sean was shorter by almost two feet, but he was fast and strong and versatile. He switched between moves on the fly, punching one second, grappling the next, and despite the difference in weight, the Medamoth couldn't muscle him.

Qoros feinted a kick at Sean's left side and then struck out with his left arm. Sean locked the fingers of his left hand on Qoros' left wrist and ducked under the Medamoth's extended arm, pressing his back against his opponent's side. For a second, it looked like Qoros was going to hug him from behind, then Sean bent his knees and did something quick with his legs and pushed back. The Medamoth went flying over Sean and landed on his back in the dirt. All the air went out of him with an audible *woosh*. Sean crouched by him, put two fingers on Qoros' throat, and got up.

I soundlessly clapped out of Qoros' sight. Sean trotted over, leaned over me, and brushed my lips with his. "That almost never works," he whispered in my ear. "Every white belt in Judo tries that move."

Qoros finally sucked some air into his lungs, coughed and sat up.

I offered Sean a sip of iced tea from my glass. He drank a long swallow.

"Good fight," Qoros said, rising. He walked over and sat in the oversized chair I had made for him.

"Thank you for sparring."

"My litter mate fought on Nexus." Qoros kept his voice casual. "He told me this legend about his commander. His name was Turan Adin. He smelled like a human, but he wasn't one. He fought like a demon on the battlefield, never tiring, never surrendering an inch of the ground he protected. He never removed his armor, and no one saw his face, but if you were in trouble during the battle and he saw you, he would carry you out. Then one day he left with the Merchants, the clan of Nuan, to help bring an end to the endless war. The war stopped, yet he never returned. Some say he died. Some say he found love and started a family. Some say he sleeps in stasis, waiting to rise again when he's needed."

It took all of my will to keep a straight face.

"That's a hell of a story," Sean said.

Qoros nodded. "One has to ask himself, what would a creature like that value most? What trait of his character made him succeed?"

"Control, probably," Sean said. "Both the Otrokar and the knights give in to their emotions. They rage. They lose themselves to the battle. They think of their fallen and their honor, and they let it fuel them on and off the battlefield. That's easy. What's hard is to maintain control in the middle of chaos. But what do I know? I'm just an innkeeper."

"Another round?" Qoros asked.

"Why not?"

They headed back to the lawn.

The inn shifted slightly. I checked the Drífen quarters. Saro had snuck onto the balcony and was trying to climb off it into the orchard. He tried to find purchase on the wall, but it was too slick. He hung off the rail, torn. Finally, he jumped. I caught him in midair with my magic and let him land by the patio. The little beast froze, shocked. He had expected to land in the orchard, and he had no idea how he wound up here.

I walked over to him. Saro saw me and shivered, a look of determination on his furry face.

"Can I help you, honored guest?" I asked gently.

The little beast blinked at me, looking as if he expected me to sprout fangs and bite his head off.

I waited.

"I lost it," he whispered in a sad tiny voice.

"What did you lose?"

"My pouch. The liege made it for me herself out of thread and I lost it. I have to find it. Don't tell."

I concentrated. The Drífen magic stained their items, and

because Gertrude Hunt didn't like it, it tried to form a protective bubble of its own power around anything Drífan. Finding a knot of magic on the stairs by the Drífan door took less than a second.

I opened my hand. A wooden tendril slid out of the wall and deposited a small purse into my hand. It was crocheted out of soft white yarn and tied with a leather cord.

Saro's eyes opened so wide, they took up half of his face.

"Is this it?" I asked.

He nodded wordlessly.

"Here." I offered the purse to the little beast.

He snatched it from my hand with its tiny paw hands, hugged it, and spun around on the lawn, his tail fluffed out. "I found it," he sang. "I found it, I found it."

"Would you like a lemon muffin?" I asked. "I won't tell."

———

Saro pulled the leather cord open and showed me the inside of the satchel. He had stuffed half of a muffin into his mouth, and his cheeks bulged out like he was a chipmunk who tried to eat a walnut.

I looked. A small chunk of wood stained with some brown crud. Perfectly ordinary.

Saro hugged the purse to him. "The old liege did my clan a big favor. When I was young, I had to come to serve him at the Red House. It's a big house on top of the mountain."

He raised his arms as far as they would go.

"Big. Many buildings. Around the buildings is a thorn fence. It obeys only the liege and it will only open to those who have a house talisman. The steward gave me a talisman and duties to go in the woods and harvest herbs and berries. There was a kurgo in the woods."

His voice dropped. Clearly the kurgo left an impression and not a good one.

"He would come up to the house and nobody would chase him off, because he had done a favor to the old lord. He didn't have a house talisman, but he would come up right to the fence and tell me I was tasty and that he would eat me."

Saro shivered.

"And the old lord tolerated this?"

"The old lord was grieving. He withdrew to his rooms and wouldn't come out. I'm a small thing. Life is hard for small things. Nobody cared. Nobody noticed me. I had to go to the woods to do my duties, and the kurgo would find me, and I would run and hide. Liege Adira had no power, she was just a cook, and everyone was mean to her, but she always let me hide in her kitchen. The kurgo would stand outside by the fence, right by the kitchen door, and scream at her to give me to him. He called her names and he told her he would kill her when she went out to the woods."

"And where was Zedas when all of this was happening?"

"Zedas is very important. Very old. He doesn't notice things unless they're important to the liege."

My opinion of Zedas plunged even lower.

"One day the kurgo caught me, bit off my finger and ate it." Saro showed me his stump. "He said I was too tasty to eat all at once. I ran real fast to the kitchen. The kurgo tried to chase me but the thorn fence wouldn't let him through. The kurgo screamed and beat his wings, and the liege Adira found me in the cupboard. And then she took a big stick and told the thorn fence to open and let her through. She had no house talisman, but the fence obeyed. The kurgo came onto the grounds, even though he was forbidden, and then she beat him with a stick. And she hit him, and hit him, and hit him."

Saro waved his tiny fists. "And the kurgo cried and called for the lord, and she hit him again until the stick broke." Saro smiled. "She gave me a piece of the broken stick, so I wouldn't be afraid anymore. It still has the kurgo's blood on it. Sometimes when I get really scared, I take it out and sniff it, and then I'm not afraid anymore."

Sean and Qoros had paused their rematch and were looking at us. They both seemed a bit disturbed.

"Do you want to sniff it?" Saro offered.

"No, thank you."

The little beast put his satchel away and reached for another muffin.

"Saro, do you know why Zedas doesn't want your liege to visit Earth?"

"The liege is the strongest on the mountain. She has many enemies. Many, many. Zedas worries that if she's off the mountain, her enemies would hurt her."

"I won't let anyone hurt her," I told him. "This inn is my mountain. I keep it safe."

The koo-ko chamber exploded.

———

I HAD BEEN WATCHING THE DEBATE, BUT SPLITTING MY ATTENTION three ways made me slightly slower, so when a small pink koo-ko vomited the silver capsule of a gas grenade, I didn't react quickly enough. By the time my brain processed the visual input, the koo-ko had compressed the capsule between his hands. A plume of purple smoke erupted. The inn screamed a warning in my head about a paralyzing agent. I blew a hole in the koo-ko chamber, venting it to the lawn, and activated the sonic attack.

A terrifying howl, like an elephant and a tiger screaming in unison, blasted into the chamber. Hearing the cry of their worst natural predator short circuited the koo-ko's brains. The predator was behind them, a hole flooded with sunlight was in front of them, and so they did what koo-ko did best. They fled.

A gaggle of koo-ko burst out onto the lawn, scattering as they ran, squawking and screeching, straight at Sean and Qoros. The Medamoth's eyes flashed. He clasped his hands into a single fist, went down to one knee, and pressed his forehead against his fingers, chanting "I will not chase, I will not chase, I will not chase, Devourer give me strength, I will not chase."

Sean planted himself next to Qoros and put his hand on the Medamoth's shoulder. I sealed the chamber, vacuumed it out, refilled the atmosphere, and launched the outdoor nets. They flew from under the roof, falling onto the koo-ko, and contracted, pulling the philosophers together into three big clumps on the grass. In a breath, it was all over.

Saro stole another muffin.

"It's over," Sean told Qoros.

The Medamoth exhaled.

"Your brother is a good soldier," Sean said. "Come on. We have places to be. We can talk on the way."

They left the lawn.

I walked over to the big balls of netted koo-kos and fixed First Scholar Thek with my innkeeper stare. He swallowed.

"I am not amused," I told him.

"Our apologies."

"You guaranteed that none of your people would bring weapons."

A root of the inn burst from the ground, holding the culprit aloft. A thin tendril wrapped around his beak, muzzling him.

"He's young," Thek gasped. "He didn't understand the consequences of his actions. We plead for mercy."

I faced the would-be assassin. "Why? What was so important?"

89

The tendril unwrapped enough to let him speak.

"The truth," he chirped. "The truth was being suppressed."

I muzzled him again and looked at Thek.

"The young one's faction had used all of their allotted time," the First Scholar explained. "They were unable to complete their argument."

"And that justified killing everyone? That is a rhetorical question. The answer is no."

"He didn't think it through," another koo-ko piped up.

"He swallowed the capsule before arriving here. That's premeditation."

"Mercy," Thek squawked.

"You don't understand the fervor of a spirited debate," a koo-ko from another cage said.

"Some debates aren't worth having."

An outraged chorus of squawks protested.

"There is always a benefit in the debate," Thek said.

"Name one debate that's not worth having," another koo-ko called out.

"What came first, the chicken or the egg?"

A stunned silence answered.

"Obviously the chicken came first," a voice called out. "Someone had to have laid the egg."

"The chicken had to have hatched from something," another koo-ko countered.

I amplified my voice to a low thunder. "It doesn't matter. No value can be gained from debating it. No benefit to society, no improvement in the quality of life or advancement of science. It's a pointless question. None of you are looking for the truth. You simply like to argue and brawl."

My captives stared at me in outrage. I had done the impossible. I had unified the koo-ko.

The young koo-ko dangled from the root, looking sad and pitiful. I could jettison him from the grounds to some terrible planet. I could put him into solitary confinement which would almost certainly drive him mad. Ultimately, half of the responsibility for this disaster rested on my shoulders. I should have scanned them more carefully when they entered, and I should have reacted faster. I wasn't an amateur. I knew the koo-ko reputation.

"I will spare him on one condition. The lot of you will go back to your chambers and debate a question of my choosing."

They murmured to each other.

"I require an answer now."

"We will save the young one," Thek said. "Ask your question."

"If it could be decided which one of your ancestors was the first founder, will your society as a whole benefit from it, and how? This is a timed debate. I will require an answer by five p.m. tomorrow."

"It is a worthy question," Thek announced. "We will debate. You will have your answer."

LIKE MOST TEXANS, I MEASURED DISTANCE IN HOURS. SAN ANTONIO was roughly three hours away. The show started taping at two, and Sean left by nine thirty. He was accompanied by two oversized combat friends, one tall, dark haired and still resembling a Polynesian, but without curly blond locks or pink eyes, and the other equally tall and heavily bearded. I warned them that small children would mistake Orro for Hagrid, which Sean found amusing.

The day proceeded with minimal emergencies. I ordered more Grand Burgers and delivered them to the Drífen. What Orro

91

didn't know wouldn't hurt him. As much as I didn't want to undercut Orro's struggle, in the end, it wasn't about Orro or his feelings. A guest had made a request, and it was within my power to grant it.

The koo-ko proceeded to debate, with the would-be assassin participating from a permanent spot in his own personal claw. I had deep scanned all of them and hadn't found any other foreign objects.

Wilmos came and delivered a massive amount of weapons. I thought of installing them but decided to wait for Sean.

I had tea with Caldenia and we watched Tom Laurent approach Peterson's spy. Tom knocked on the window until the man rolled it down.

"Are you vice?" Tom demanded.

"No," the spy said.

"Are you here surveilling my wife?"

"Buddy, I don't know who your wife is."

Tom squinted at the spy. "I know you can deny being a cop if you're undercover. Listen, if you are building a case against my wife, I've got her on film. I have all of her *visitors* on video. And you may want to tell your buddies in narcotics that they might be doing meth in there. It's sex and drugs. The more charges the better."

The spy stared at him.

"I'll testify, I'll wear a wire."

"Sir, what the hell are you talking about?"

"I'm fighting for custody here. Throw me a bone."

Officer Marais chose this moment to pull up behind the spy in his cruiser. The spy took off and Tom proceeded to tell Marais his tale of woe. Marais listened to him for about five minutes and informed him that who his wife chose to let into her home and how that affected her rights to custody was a matter for family court. If he suspected drug use, he was welcome to file a report online. Tom moved on and after a while Marais did too.

At six p.m. I served the dinner Orro had prepped and texted Sean to see if he was okay. He texted back OMW and nothing else.

I tried to read, then I tried to watch TV, then I walked back and forth through the inn, and by the time his car pulled into the driveway, I had worried myself into being a basket case.

I watched the three of them get out of the car. Everyone still had the right number of appendages. They were fine. Of course they were fine. I'd worried for nothing. I met them as they entered the front room. Sean's face radiated controlled fury.

Uh oh.

Sean pointed down the hall. The humanizer illusion collapsed and Orro took off at an alarming speed. Qoros patted Sean's shoulder and went to his rooms. Sean collapsed into a chair.

"So, how did it go?" I was almost afraid to ask.

Sean made a fart noise.

"Did Qoros make a scene at the Alamo?"

Sean shook his head.

"You're killing me. What is it? What happened?"

He passed a tiny data card to me. I tossed it at the nearest wall. It swallowed it and a huge screen appeared, playing a recording. Sean, Qoros, and Orro sat in chairs. The angle of the recording suggested a camera hovering high above them from the side. Sean must have launched a surveillance unit. It was about the size of a walnut and it was programed to hide, a fly on the proverbial wall.

The show started. I had no idea how they even managed to get in on such short notice.

On stage Garry Keys chopped vegetables like his life depended on it, lecturing about the benefits of organic produce and purple carrots. The show was filmed in spurts, allowing for commercial breaks. At times a stagehand stopped Garry to tell him something

93

or to adjust something in the shot. Orro fidgeted in his seat, leaning forward, fascinated, making chopping motions with his hands. The sight of Sean bookended by two giant, somewhat freaky-looking humans was slightly comical.

Garry Keys finished sautéing his vegetables, placed the duck in the oven, and a commercial break was called. An assistant blotted Garry's forehead. Another assistant took the raw duck out of the oven and replaced it with a perfectly roasted bird. Garry waved at him. The assistant brought the cooked duck over. Garry examined it critically and made a comment. The assistant produced a bottle of soy sauce and a brush. He strategically painted the bird, darkening the skin. Garry examined it again, gave it two thumbs up, and it went back into the oven. Meanwhile, another assistant replaced the pot with vegetables.

Orro stared at the stage. The humanizer did its best to mimic emotions, but I couldn't tell what Orro was feeling. He looked like a deer in headlights.

The break ended and taping resumed. Garry made a great show of pulling the duck out of the oven. "And here we are. Would you look at that? Fire and lightning!"

A stagehand held up a cue card with "Applause" on it. The studio audience *oohed* and clapped enthusiastically.

Orro surged to his feet and roared, "You are a fraud!"

Oh my God.

Sean grabbed him, trying to pull him back into his seat, but Orro threw him off.

"You are no chef! That poultry is a lie!"

Garry spun around, looking for the offender, saw an outraged giant, and started backing up.

"You dare!" Orro sputtered, jabbing his shovel hand in Garry's direction.

Security converged on the row, moving in.

"You're not fit to cook dog food, you vile pretender!" Orro roared.

Sean smashed his hand against Orro's temple, too high to do any real damage if Orro was a human, but right where a Quillonian's left ear would be. Orro crumpled. Qoros heaved him over his shoulder like Orro weighed nothing. Sean took off, the Medamoth right behind him. Sean and the security team collided at the end of the row. There was a scuffle, legs and arms flew as bodies were knocked to the ground, and Sean and Qoros fled the studio, carrying Orro like a sack of potatoes. The camera streaked after them and the feed ended.

I rubbed my face. "Did they call the cops?"

"No," Sean said. "I was very careful. I just tripped a couple of them. Nobody was hurt."

Except Orro.

"Did you talk to him?"

"We tried. He won't respond. He didn't say a word on the ride back."

"I'll go talk to him."

Sean nodded. "You were right. It was a bad idea."

"You did the best you could. And … it might be for the best. I keep telling him not to trust everything on TV and he never listens. Did Qoros get what he wanted, at least?"

Sean nodded. "He wanted to know how to prevent a war with the Hope-Crushing Horde."

"What did you tell him?"

Sean sighed. "The truth. They will fight their enemy to the bitter end, but they will give the shirt off their back to their friend. The only way to avoid a war with the Otrokars is to earn their friendship."

I walked down the hallway, past the atrium filled with Orro's prized herbs, to a green door. I knocked. "Can I come in?"

"Yes," a dull voice answered.

I opened the door and entered the room. Orro's suite was made by him. He showed me what he wanted, and I reproduced it as faithfully as I could. It was the room of a sentient creature, but it felt like the cozy den of some small animal. The rooms had no sharp angles. The soft eggshell walls met the floor and the ceiling with a curve, as if the space had been hollowed out of a log or dug out of forest soil. The doorways were arched, the large window slightly misshapen, neither a circle nor a square. African violets in cute pots lived on the windowsill. The furniture was large, plush, and curved. A huge TV took up most of one wall, and bookshelves filled with books, scrolls, tablets, and other media in a dozen galactic languages, lined the other.

In the middle of all of this Orro curled on the blue rug, a sagging heap of quills. I couldn't even see his head.

I sat next to him and patted his back.

"He was a fraud," Orro whispered.

"I'm so sorry."

"He lied."

"Maybe. He probably is a good chef, and his recipes are sound. But it's a TV show. It's made to entertain. It would have taken him at least two and a half hours to roast that duck."

"He should have done it. Instead he brought a duck he didn't cook and tried to pass it off as his own. He painted it with soy sauce."

"I'm so sorry. Why do you think he did that?"

Orro bit off his words. "So it would look better."

"Exactly. It's TV. It can't convey to you how things smell or how they taste. It can only show you how good they look. It has to be entertaining. Not many people would sit there and watch him roast a duck for two hours."

"I would."

He was heartbroken and I didn't know what to do.

"You didn't go there to be entertained. You went there for the food, because you are a great chef, Orro."

"Do you want me to pack?" he asked softly.

"Why would you have to pack?"

"I broke my word. I dishonored my combat friends. I made a scene."

I hugged him. Quills poked me. "No, I don't want you to pack. You're my friend, Orro. You're always welcome here. This is your home for as long as you want it."

He sniffled.

"Besides, you're a great chef. All the other inns envy me. Where else would I find a chef this amazing?"

He sniffled again. "I'm a better chef than Garry Keys."

"That was never in doubt."

E arly the next morning, I knocked on the frame of Adira's window. She stood with her back to me, reading a long scroll, but the sound hadn't startled her. She turned slowly, smiled at me, and said, "Come in."

I moved the glass and walked in. Adira looked at the plain grey robe in my hands.

"Are you busy?" I asked.

"Not particularly."

"Have you ever been to Baha-char?"

Adira frowned. "No."

"Then I propose that you and I go shopping, and then go have brunch at Baha-char."

Adira looked at me, looked at the robe, and then looked at me again. "What kind of shopping is available at Baha-char?"

"Every kind."

Adira took the robe and called out, "Imur, if Zedas asks, I am resting and am not to be disturbed."

"Yes, my liege," A female voice answered from the main bedroom.

Adira pulled the robe on and followed me out the window. We slid to the first floor, went inside, down the hallway, and to a door.

"What's in the satchel?" Adira nodded at a large tattered bag on my shoulder.

"I have to run an errand to help a friend. It won't take long."

"Will the inn be alright without you?"

"My boyfriend will take care of it. He's installing extra weapons for your meeting."

Adira smiled as if I had said something amusing.

The door swung open and sunshine flooded the hallway.

"What is this?" Adira asked.

"Come with me and find out."

We walked the sunlit streets of Baha-char under the purple sky, while the broken planet rose slowly above us. We gawked at strange creatures, ducked into little shops, and bargained with the shop keepers. I took her to the Fiber Row, where all things thread, fabric, and yarn were sold. She walked into a store the size of Wal-Mart filled with skeins of yarn in every color and didn't leave for two hours. She bought yarn, or rather I bought it for her and she promised to reimburse me. I bought a short sword for Sean at a small stall a few streets over. It seemed very old, made of a strange dark blue metal, but razor sharp.

Afterward, tired, we sat at a small café, guarding the big sack of yarn and my sword with our legs, while a waitress with four arms brought us tall drinks filled with green liquid and bubbles. The bubbles would break free and burst with a loud pop, making the air smell like persimmons.

Somewhere between the first table of yarn and my sword purchase, Adira turned human. She smiled, and talked, and there was life in her face.

"What made you want to invite me?" she asked, sipping her drink.

"You seemed sad."

"I was sad."

"You can open a portal to Baha-char from your system," I told her. "Baha-char is much easier to reach than Earth, and I know that other Dryhten visit it for trade. You can come here whenever you want." I reached into my satchel and pulled out a small wooden amulet, a branch of striated wood braided into a circle. I handed it to her. "The entrance for Gertrude Hunt is in the alley by the Saurian merchant. He sells underwater lights. It's the only shop of its kind at Baha-char. If you go down the alley to its end with this amulet in hand, Gertrude Hunt will let me know. You can visit whenever you want."

"It's a shortcut?"

"Yes, it is." I smiled at her. "You promised Zedas that you wouldn't open a portal to Earth. You didn't say anything about Baha-char. He is an Akeraat. He will appreciate your cleverness."

"Thank you." Adira slipped the amulet into her robe. Her face turned grave. "Tonight, my uncle comes."

"We will be ready. I'll make sure you will have privacy."

Adira's expression turned sharper. "I don't want privacy."

"You don't?" I thought this was a family matter and an awkward one at that.

"I want to meet him outside. I want everyone to see it, so every word is witnessed. I'll be making a statement."

"Very well." I'd planned to make a special room, but I could move it outside, behind the inn.

"When the time comes," Adira said, "I don't want you to worry about my safety. Concentrate on protecting the inn and the other guests instead."

"You don't want me to interfere."

"It wouldn't be fair to you. I regret involving you in this. I hope your power will be enough to contain what is to come."

"And that doesn't sound ominous, not at all." I sipped my drink.

"Dina, it can't all be sunshine, shopping trips, and bubbly drinks."

"But wouldn't it be nice if it was?"

We left the café and walked down a winding street to a large restaurant. A line of beings stretched out the door. I approached the creature by the door, a big beefy beast with a ferocious face and fangs as big as fingers.

"I have a parcel for Chef Adri."

The beast glared at me. "Chef Adri doesn't cook here."

"I didn't say he did."

I opened my satchel and took out a clear plastic container. Inside the container, secured by tiny prongs, sat a lemon muffin. A folded piece of paper waited next to the muffin. I handed it to the door beast, and we left.

"I had fun," Adira said when we reached the alley. "Is there anything I can do for you in return?"

"It's not necessary," I told her. "I didn't do it for a favor. I did it because it made me happy."

———

RUDOLPH PETERSON ARRIVED AT FOUR THIRTY. HE EXITED THE CAR, flanked by two bodyguards in suits, and attempted to make his way up the driveway. He got two feet in before I turned the air toxic. After the three of them got done coughing their lungs out, they retreated to the car to wait.

I visited the koo-ko, informed them that the debate had to stop until the end of Adira's meeting, relayed Adira's request, and bribed them with an extra hour to finish their debate and a giant TV screen so they could watch the meeting. I created a gallery on the back wall of the inn, an armored room shielded by three feet of clear crystasteel, and invited Caldenia, Orro, and Qoros into it. When I left it, Caldenia and Qoros were chatting like old friends and complimenting Orro on the hors d'oeuvres he'd whipped up.

Sean had gone to the war room. My original plan was to join him there, but Adira asked me to sit with her. I had the absurd feeling that a duel was coming, and I would be her second.

I moved a table and three chairs out of storage and set them a hundred feet from the kitchen door. Gertrude Hunt had been spreading its roots, claiming the land I'd purchased, and my power extended over the three acres directly behind the inn. I hoped it would be enough.

At four fifty my cell phone rang. Mr. Rodriguez, Tony's father. I answered.

"I called to wish you good luck," he told me.

"How did you know?"

"She's broadcasting it."

What? "How?"

"I don't know. But it's on the main screen across every inn."

I groaned.

"Do your best," Mr. Rodriguez said.

"You don't understand." The nervous doubt that had been curling inside me broke free. "Ever since I came back from the death of the seed, there is this distance between me and the inn. It's like the inn is holding back."

"Dina, you have no time. Listen to me, I don't know what you're feeling, but the inns are like dogs. They give themselves completely. They don't know how to hold back. You will do fine. You have my full confidence."

He hung up.

He was right. The inns didn't know how to hold back.

It was me.

The Drífen were coming down the staircase. I had only three minutes to spare.

I closed my eyes and opened my soul. The doubt, the guilt, the fear, I let it go, and Gertrude Hunt's magic flooded into me, clean and strong. The past already happened; the future was now. I was an innkeeper, this was my inn, and everything and everyone within it was in my care.

I opened my eyes, folded space, and let the Drífen exit onto the back lawn.

The five retainers took positions on the back porch. Adira walked to the table alone and sat. She still wore her old cloak. Still ordinary.

I walked to the front door, opened it, and stepped outside in my robe. Rudolph Peterson saw me and charged up the driveway. He was halfway to the door before he realized his bodyguards hadn't made it. He glanced over his shoulder at two men suddenly confronted with a wall of boiling hot air.

"Just you," I told him.

He waved them off and they got back into the car.

I led him around the back, through the gate in the fence, to the table. He sat across from Adira. I took the chair between them.

There was a pitcher of iced tea on the table and three glasses. Adira drank from hers. Her uncle grabbed the pitcher and poured himself a glass.

An electric tension vibrated through me, not really nervousness, but anticipation. Something was going to happen.

"You look good," Rudolph said. "You look like your mother."

Adira drank some more of her tea.

"I tried to help her. I really did, but you know how she was."

"My mother died five years ago. She suffered for a long time. I was there when she called you for help and you said no."

Rudolph's hands curled into fists. "I asked her for a simple thing. Just one thing, the only favor I ever asked. I would have given her everything for that."

"Did you summon me here to alleviate your guilt?" Adira asked. "I can do no more than my mother could to grant your wish."

Rudolph slapped a hand on the table and bared his teeth. "She didn't want to. She was selfish her entire life."

Adira waited, her expression placid. Some of the rage went out of Rudolph's eyes.

"When you and my mother were sixteen, you went on a hike and somewhere on that mountain path you left Earth and entered Chatune. It opened to you, because it recognized the dormant power within you. You were meant for great things, but you squandered the gift Chatune offered, uncle. You schemed and plotted, trying to rise through the imperial ranks based not on scholarship, military art, or the cultivation of your inner power, but on trickery and deceit. You lied, misled, and betrayed."

"I was at a disadvantage. I had no family, no connections, no backing. We came to that world with nothing except the clothes on our backs and two backpacks. I was trying to build a secure future for me and for your mother." Rudolph tapped the table with his finger. "I got the raw end of that deal. I only had crumbs of your mother's magic. She got the lion's share and I had to make do with the leftovers."

"My mother failed as well," Adira said. "The Mountain reached out to her, trying to forge a connection. Mother understood what was required of her. The Mountain wanted a protector, and instead of answering that call, my mother rebuffed it. She flittered through the world like a butterfly without care. You wanted position and power, and she wanted attention and admiration...No, adoration is a better word. She played with people's emotions like they were marbles, and when she recognized that there were consequences, she fled the world that had taken her in."

"Exactly!" Rudolph leaned forward. "I'm so glad you understand. She chose to leave. She chose to come back here. But I was expelled when she left. I can't go back on my own. I require your mother to open the door for me."

"Why do you think that is?" Adira asked.

"Why does it matter? I worked for ten years to build something. I was an advisor. I had power, I had wealth, and she, that stupid bitch, took it all away from me. I begged her to go back. Begged. I had to start all over and on her deathbed, riddled with cancer, she still refused. She claimed she tried and couldn't enter. And then she disappeared, and I knew she lied. She went back to Chatune and took you instead of me."

"It matters because you still don't understand." Adira set her glass down. "My mother didn't lie. She truly couldn't return to Chatune, with you or without. Each of you on your own weren't enough. The two of you were supposed to work together, but you failed, and Chatune didn't want you or her anymore. My mother had to offer something to buy her passage. She offered me. For the sake of obtaining me, Chatune permitted her to tag along. My mother didn't tell me what she was doing. She didn't care about me or my life. She thought Chatune would cure her, but it let her rot, and I took care of her until she died, selfish to the end. Do you see, uncle? You hold no value to Chatune. It doesn't want you."

Rudolph recoiled.

"You talk about that damn planet like it has a soul."

Adira laughed. It sounded bitter.

Rudolph's face melted into an earnest expression. He probably had no idea how fake it looked. "You're right. Your mother was selfish to the end. But you don't have to be. The liege lord of the Green Mountain adopted you as his daughter. He shared his power with you. Take me back with you."

She smiled. "Why?"

Rudolph leaned forward again. "You're my niece. I'm the only family you have left. I was a powerful man before Chatune spat me out. Take me with you, and I'll help you rise. I will take care of you."

"You are a powerful man here, uncle. You have everything you could possibly want. Stay here."

"Adira…"

"No."

The final no landed like a brick between us. The silence stretched, oppressive.

"None of it matters." Rudolph bared his teeth again, his face almost a grimace. "You have magic, so you don't know what it's like to lose it. You could share that world with me, but you won't. You're just like your mother, an egotistical, self-centered bitch. It doesn't matter. I've done my part. I will get to Chatune without you."

The far end of the grounds shimmered, as if hot air burst from the grass. Reality ceased to be, as if someone had sliced through our world with a knife, and beyond it a vast green valley spread. A warrior strode onto the grass. He was tall and clad in black armor embossed with gold. His face was inhumanly beautiful, his long white hair braided and pulled into a ponytail. He carried a sword that was five feet long and engraved with strange symbols.

It was like a scene from a movie. Magnificent and shocking.

The blast wave of the warrior's magic tore across the lawn, snapping every blade of grass upright, and met my power. I swallowed it and dispersed it. So much magic…

"Liege Yastreb of the Onyx Sect." Adira set her glass down.

"You sold me out, uncle. You sent that message to lure me from the Mountain, to here, where I would be vulnerable."

"You left me no choice," he spat.

Behind the warrior other armored soldiers materialized like shadows coming into focus. So many soldiers…

"You're wrong. There's always a choice. You just didn't like it." Adira smiled. "When I received your message, I asked myself how a human could send a letter to Chatune. I asked myself what you could possibly want. The answer was obvious."

Rudolph blanched. "You knew."

"Of course. Yastreb approached you and promised you passage to Chatune for your betrayal. What's about to happen isn't about you. It's about me making a statement to all those who think I require the Mountain to defend what is mine." Adira rose. "Keep an eye on my uncle, innkeeper. Don't let him come to any harm."

Sean's voice sounded in my ear. "Ready."

I snapped the void field in place. The highest-level barrier available to an innkeeper, the void field stopped organic and inorganic projectiles and the transfer of energy. I had bubbled three acres; the warrior, his army, the inn, and the portal. The void field prevented any sound from passing through. Now it was just a matter of holding it.

We had discussed our strategy beforehand. Sean and I would defend the inn together.

Adira walked in front of the table.

Yastreb glared at her from across the lawn. His voice was like thunder. "Submit."

Adira lifted her chin, her voice casual and light. "Not today."

She raised her hands, fingers open, as if preparing to catch a basketball, and drew them apart, removing an invisible scabbard. A sword appeared in her right hand, a slender double-edged blade, a full four feet long. Silver fangs protruded from its guard, and its pommel was shaped like a snarling female lion.

Yastreb's face jerked.

"Not the sword you were expecting?" Adira asked. "I don't need the Heart of the Mountain for you. The Lion Fang will do just fine."

The warrior's black blade burst into blue fire. Magic tore out of him, sheathing him in a dense armor of power. His soldiers charged, streaming past him into two dark currents.

Adira's inner power erupted. Magic punched me, sweeping my defenses aside. I couldn't breathe, I couldn't move, and for a second I thought I died. Her cloak tore and fell, shredded. She wore green armor that clung to her like a second skin. Red hungry fire bathed her blade.

Rudolph started to get up.

"Move and die," I told him, my voice flat.

He sat back down.

Adira *moved*.

I had seen incredible swordsmen fight. During the peace summit, an arbitrator brought a genius swordswoman to my inn. Her name was Sophie and she killed with such beauty and precision that it transformed it into art. For her, the connection she felt with her opponent just before life became death meant everything.

For Adira it meant nothing. This wasn't art; it was raw elemental force.

The soldiers rushed her, each a single storm of magic. She moved her sword, and they died, torn apart by her magic, like paper tigers burnt to ash. Magic hammered the void field, splashing against it. I grit my teeth. The entire barrage of the Draziri at their strongest didn't have a third of this impact.

A soldier skirted Adira and ran at me. Sean's kel-rifle fired with a twang and he collapsed.

More and more soldiers came, rushing around Adira, trying to swarm her. She killed them without noticing, oblivious to their attacks, intent only on walking toward their commander. There were so many of them, they got into each other's way like ants climbing over each other to bite a grasshopper. Those on the periphery of the swarm turned to me. They couldn't get to Adira, but they recognized I was her ally, and they rushed me, weapons and magic ready. Sean's guns boomed, once, twice, and pounded into a steady beat as he pulverized them into nothing.

Yastreb ran forward, accelerating, the dark mantle of his magic flowing around him.

I planted my broom into the dirt. It split, glowing with pale blue, a conduit to Gertrude Hunt, fusing us into one.

Adira cut down the last of the soldiers directly between her and Yastreb and sprinted.

The two Drífen collided.

BOOM.

A shock wave of magic rippled through the inn's grounds. Soldiers flew, rag dolls tossed in the air.

The magic seared me. I tasted blood in my mouth.

The void field held.

Adira slid across the lawn, driven back by the pressure of the Onyx warrior's sword. She leaned out of the way by some miracle, spun with impossible grace, and slashed at Yastreb. He parried.

BOOM. Another blast of magic. Heat and pressure crushed me. I clenched my teeth and held.

Roots slithered underground, surfaced, and wrapped around my legs. Branches burst from the wall, stretching to me, winding around my shoulders. I sat ensconced in Gertrude Hunt, and through the inn, I felt Sean on the other end.

We connected.

The lawn turned into a slaughterhouse. Sean rained death onto the battlefield, his weapons chewing through the mass of soldiers trying to lessen the impact of their magic on the void field. Adira and the warrior clashed like two gods not caring what they destroyed. And I contained it all, holding this hell on Earth between my hands.

Yastreb was slowing down. He bled from two places, where her sword had caught him, but Adira showed no signs of fatigue. She cut at him, tireless, each strike amplified by her magic.

The flood of soldiers ended. I almost didn't notice. My eyes were bleeding and it felt like I had gone deaf, but somehow, I could still hear.

Adira kicked at Yastreb. He was a fraction of a second too slow to dodge. Her foot connected with his chest. He stumbled back, out of breath. She chased him, reached out, and gripped the warrior by his throat. His magic bit at her, but she didn't care. She jerked him up and neatly slid him onto her sword.

Yastreb screamed. Magic boomed, the sound of a god dying. Adira freed her sword with a sharp tug and kicked the bleeding warrior in the chest. He flew across the lawn back into the portal. She waved her hand and the gap between two worlds snapped shut.

I let the void field drain down. Everything hurt, but the sudden loss of pressure felt like heaven.

It was so quiet.

Around us bodies began to sink into the soil, as the inn claimed the dead.

Next to me Rudolph Peterson stared at Adira, his face a mask of disbelief.

She walked to us, her sword, no longer on fire, resting on her shoulder.

"Today the Mountain stood firm," she said, speaking to nobody in particular. "Those who covet what is ours take note. Think carefully before you trespass for the Mountain will not spare you."

She turned to Rudolph. He was looking at her like she was the Grim Reaper.

"Do you understand now, uncle? The lord of the Green Mountain didn't share his power with me. This power is my own. This is what you and my mother were meant to be."

He opened his mouth, but nothing came out.

Adira turned to me. "Well done, innkeeper. The Green Mountain owes you a debt. I had asked you about mercy. I remember your answer. My uncle is my only family by blood. He is all that ties me to this world. Before I left the Mountain, I made a vow to the ancestors of my dryht. I promised that I would either forgive him and walk away with a clean soul or that I would kill him in a way he deserves and I would make it so violent and brutal that his death would be an enduring example to our enemies."

Rudolph just stared, shell-shocked.

"This man in front of you has seen what you can do," Adira continued. "If I spare him, he will never leave you alone. He will pursue you with all of the resources available to him, because he hungers for the power you and I possess. He is a wealthy man. Someone will come looking for him. If I kill him in a way I vowed, you won't be able to explain his death. If I take him with me and kill him on the Mountain, you won't be able to explain his disappearance. I've asked too much of you already. I will break my vow today. It is a weight I will have to bear. You are a good person and I will show you mercy. Please accept my sacrifice."

The sword in Adira's hand turned transparent, a ghost of itself. Gracefully, elegantly, she swung and plunged it into her uncle's chest. Rudolph Peterson froze, his mouth a gaping O. Adira freed her blade and he fell softly onto the grass.

"I stopped his heart," she told me. "He died a natural death and left behind an intact corpse."

"So much more than he deserved," the white woman said from the porch. I had forgotten Adira's guards were even there.

Zedas bowed, intoning the words. "Thank you, Liege of Green Mountain, for this lesson in compassion."

The four other retainers bowed.

Adira waved her fingers, melting the sword into nothing, picked up the pitcher of iced tea and drained it.

EPILOGUE

After the battle, Sean had come to get me. I'd had trouble walking and he supported me until we got into the house and then he carried me upstairs. He helped me undress and lowered me into a bathtub of hot soapy water. I asked him to make sure everyone was back in their rooms and supervise the cleanup. He growled about leaving me by myself, but in the end he went.

I washed the blood off my face and sat in the soap bubbles until my head stopped humming and my teeth no longer rattled in my jaw. At some point, I crawled out, tried to dry myself off, and fell asleep on the bed wrapped in a wet towel. The last thing I remembered was putting the body of Rudolph Peterson into stasis to prevent decay. Tonight, after everyone celebrated, I would call 911 and put on a show.

I woke up an hour later. Sean was on the bed with me, resting his head on his bent arm.

"Hey," I said.

"Hey."

"Any news?"

His wolf eyes shone at me. "The Assembly sent over a message through Tony. Apparently, they watched the show and decided they didn't need to see us anymore. Overall, it seems our performance was 'satisfactory.'"

I rolled my eyes. "Satisfactory, my ass."

Sean grinned at me. "That's my line."

"I'd like to see any of them contain two Drífen lieges fighting." I rolled over and snuggled to him.

"How are you feeling?" he asked.

"Sore. And my head hurts. It was so much power. Did I scare you?"

"A little. The inn didn't freak out, so I knew you weren't too hurt. You were awesome."

"We were awesome. It's we now." I glanced at him. "It's not too late to back out of being an innkeeper, you know. You could still go off and be a werewolf of adventure."

"Nah. I'm good." He kissed me.

The anxious cloud that had hung over me since the Assembly had issued their summons vanished. They could send all the summons they wanted. I didn't care. This was my inn and Sean loved me.

Half an hour later, we came down for the Treaty Stay banquet, and I wore my Treaty Stay robe, silver with a pink trim. I had a silver robe for Sean too, but all of the magic in the world couldn't force him into it. He wore jeans and a black sweater and threatened to switch to pajamas if I made a fuss. He didn't own any pajamas as far as I knew, and I made a note to buy him some.

The foxglove tree bloomed. It was a riot of color, lavender, white, and pink, every branch dripping with huge blossoms, as if Gertrude Hunt had poured its magic into the tree to celebrate. Tables had been set in the Grand Ballroom, brimming with food.

Orro had cooked so much, I was afraid the furniture might break under the weight of all those dishes.

The Grand Ballroom buzzed with many voices. The Drifen took the far table, where they sat relaxed, making jokes. The danger had clearly passed. The Medamoth had joined Caldenia at our table, and the koo-ko occupied the two remaining long tables, adjusted for their size. Qoros clearly had trouble with their darting and I heard Caldenia offer him a tranquilizer, although I wasn't sure whether it was to calm his nerves or to drug a koo-ko. I could totally picture her Grace whispering into his big ear, "There are so many. Surely nobody would miss just one. Or two." I kept counting the koo-ko just in case.

The philosophers presented me with a five-thousand-word opinion on the question I had posed, the summary of which amounted to "It doesn't matter who was the first founder, it is the debate itself that has value, for through the debate the truth will be distilled." I decided to take it, because arguing with them would only give them an excuse to debate some more, and then nobody would get to have dinner.

Magic chimed. Ah, finally. I opened the Baha-char door and tracked the visitor as he made his way down the hall. I leaned to Sean. "Could you keep an eye on them for a minute?"

He nodded, looked at Caldenia and Qoros, and gave them a hard stare. Her Grace wriggled her fingers at him. Qoros put his hand on his chest, pretending to be shocked.

I stepped out into the hallway. A large figure emerged from the soft gloom, a Quillonian, so old, his quills had turned pure white.

I bowed. "Thank you for accepting my invitation, Grand Chef."

"After that muffin, how could I not? Is he expecting me?"

"He has no idea."

"How did you find me? The apprenticeships of the Red Cleaver chefs are a closely guarded secret."

"When I invited Orro into the inn, I ran a complete background check. On the day he sent out the soup that ruined his career, you entered a period of mourning. You were in seclusion for six months. Only a devastating event would have caused you to abstain from your art for so long."

Chef Adri nodded. "He is my brightest pupil."

I led the elder Quillonian into the hall. In the center of the banquet floor, Orro held a platter of rolls, looking for a spot on the far table. He turned and saw us. His hands shook.

Chef Adri smiled.

Orro dropped the platter onto the table and fell to his knees. Chef Adri rushed to him and picked him up.

"None of that."

"Master..."

"Today there are two masters here. I have come to learn from you, my former pupil. Share with me what you have discovered. I cannot wait to taste your food."

It took another couple of minutes to get Chef Adri seated, primarily because Orro couldn't find a chair worthy enough. Finally, everyone took their places. I rose and looked over the banquet hall, the guests who would leave, the friends who would stay, and I was grateful to be exactly where I was.

The lanterns flared gently. A shower of pale petals rained from the ceiling. Soft music filled the room.

I smiled and said, my voice carrying through the inn, "Welcome to the Treaty Stay."

The End.

SNEAK PEEK OF EMERALD BLAZE

PROLOGUE

The wolf was coming.

Lander Morton knew this because he'd invited the wolf into his home. His body man, Sheldon, had come to tell him the wolf was at the door and had gone to fetch him. Now the two of them were coming back, but Lander only heard one set of footsteps echo through the house.

Lander shifted in his wheelchair and took a long swallow of his bourbon. Fire rolled down his throat. His old guts would make him pay for it later, but he didn't care. Some men were men, and others were wolves in human skin. He needed a human wolf for this job, and he would get one.

For the first time in the last three days he felt something other than crushing grief. The new emotion cut through the thick fog of despair, and he recognized it as anticipation. No, it was more than that. It was a heady mix of expectation, apprehension, and excitement tinged with fear. He used to feel like this years ago on the verge of closing a huge deal. It had been decades since he'd experienced the splash of adrenaline like this and for a moment, he felt young again.

Sheldon appeared in the doorway of the study and stood aside, letting the other man enter. The guest took three steps inside and stopped, letting himself be seen. He was young, so young, and he moved with an easy grace that made Lander feel ancient. Strong, tall, handsome in that Mediterranean way, shaped by sun and saltwater. When Felix's boy grew up, he might look like that.

Pain lashed him, and Lander struggled with it.

His guest waited.

Lander looked at his face. There it was, in the eyes, the wolf looking back at him. Cold. *Hungry.*

About time he got here. No, he couldn't say that. He had to be civil. He couldn't fuck this up. "Thank you for coming to see me on such short notice."

Sheldon stepped back into the hall and closed the doors. He would wait by them to make sure they wouldn't be interrupted.

"Please think nothing of it," the guest said. "My condolences."

Lander nodded to the bottle of Blood Oath Pact bourbon waiting on a corner of the desk. "A drink?"

The guest shook his head. "I don't drink on the job."

"Smart." Lander splashed another inch of bourbon into his glass. He wasn't sure if he was drowning his grief or building up liquid courage. If he failed to state his case and the man walked away... He couldn't let him walk away.

"I knew your father," Lander said. "I met him and your mother while I was over there making a deal for Carrara marble for Castle Hotel. It was expensive as hell, but I wanted the best."

The man shrugged.

Panic squirmed through Lander. Words came tumbling out. "They killed my son. They took his money, they used his knowledge and connections, and then they murdered him, and I don't know why."

"Do you care why?"

"Yes, but I've already hired someone for that."

"So, what do you want from me?"

"I love my son. He is smart, sharp, sharper than I ever was, and he's honest. People hate my guts, but everyone likes him because he's a good man. His wife, Sofia, died three years ago, and he takes care of his kids by himself. Two sons and a daughter. The oldest is fourteen years old. I've had a stroke, and now there's cancer eating at me, but now I can't croak for four more years. I've got to hold on until the oldest boy is old enough to take over. I want those bastards to die!"

Lander clenched his fists. He voice had gone hoarse and some part of him warned him he sounded unhinged. But the hurt was too raw, and it bled out of him.

"I want them to suffer, and I want them to know why. They took my son from me and from his children. They've ruined my boy, my handsome smart boy. Everything I built, everything he built, they think they can just rip it all away from me." His voice dropped barely above whisper, rough and dripping pain. "Kill them. Kill them for me."

Silence filled the study.

Worry drowned Lander. Had he said too much? Did he sound too crazy?

"My father died, but my mother remembers meeting you," the guest said. "There is a photo of the three of you on the yacht. She was pregnant with me at the time. She said her morning sickness was unbearable and you told her that ginger ale was the best for upset stomachs. There was no ginger ale to be had and you ordered a case of it from Milan by courier."

The guest stepped up to the desk, splashed a finger of bourbon into the second glass and raised it. "To your son."

He drained the glass in one swallow and Lander saw the wolf again, staring at him from within the man's soul.

"Does this mean you'll take the job?"

"Yes."

The relief was almost overwhelming. Lander slumped in his chair.

"I've reviewed your situation prior to my visit," the guest said. "It will take time and money. It will be complicated, because it has to be done right."

"Whatever it takes," Lander said. He felt so tired now. He'd done it. He could look at Felix's gravestone now and he could promise his son that revenge was coming.

"The proof of their guilt must be irrefutable."

"Don't worry about that," Lander said. "You'll have your proof. I only hire the best."

CHAPTER 1

"House Baylor Investigative Agency," I shouted. "Holster your weapons and step away from the monkey!"

The orange tamarin monkey stared at me from the top of the lamp post, silhouetted against the bright blue sky of a late afternoon. The two men and a woman under the post continued to grip their guns.

All three wore casual clothes, the men in khakis and T-shirts, the woman in white capris and a pale blue blouse. All three were in good shape, and they held their guns in nearly identical positions, with their barrels pointing slightly down, which marked them as professionals who didn't want to accidentally shoot us.

Given that none of us had drawn weapons yet, they must have felt they had the upper hand. Sadly for them, their assessment of their personal safety was wildly off the mark.

Next to me, Leon bared his teeth. "Catalina, I really don't like when people point guns at me."

Neither did I, but unlike Leon, I would be highly unlikely to shoot each of them through the left eye "for symmetry reasons."

"Montgomery International Investigations," the older of the men announced. "Pack it in and head back to the mystery machine, kids."

Usually Augustine's people wore suits but chasing monkeys through the sweltering inferno of Houston's July called for a more casual attire. Leon and I had opted for the casual as well. My face was dirty, my dark hair was piled in a messy bun on top of my head, and my clothes wouldn't impress anyone. Of the three of us, only Cornelius looked decent, and even he was drenched in sweat.

"You're interfering with our lawful recovery," I announced. "Step aside."

The female agent stepped forward. She was in her thirties, fit, with light brown skin and glossy dark hair pulled into a ponytail.

"You seem like a nice girl."

You have no idea.

She kept going. "Let's be reasonable about this before the testosterone starts flying. This monkey is the property of House Thom. It's a part of a very important pharmaceutical trial. I don't know what you've been told, but we have a certificate identifying the ownership of the monkey. I'll be happy to let you verify it for yourself. You're still young, so a word of advice, always get the proper paperwork to cover your ass."

"Oh no, she didn't," Leon muttered under his breath.

At twenty-one, most of my peers were either in college,

working for their House, or enjoying the luxury carefree lifestyle the powerful magic of their families provided. Being underestimated worked in my favor. However, we'd been looking for the monkey for several days. I was hot, tired, and hungry and my patience was in short supply. Besides, she insulted my paperwork skills. Paperwork was my middle name.

"This monkey is a helper monkey, a highly trained service animal, certified to assist individuals with spinal cord injuries. She was snatched from her rightful owner during a trip to the doctor and illegally sold to your client. I have her pedigree report, immunization records, vet records, certificate from the Faces, Paws, and Tail non-profit that trained her, signed affidavit from her owner, a copy of the police report, and her DNA profile. Also, I'm not a nice girl. I *am* the Head of my House conducting a lawful recovery of stolen property. Do not impede me again."

On my left Cornelius frowned. "Could we hurry this along? Rosebud is experiencing a lot of stress."

"You heard the animal mage," Leon called out. "Don't we all want what's best for the stressed-out monkey?"

The shorter of the men squinted at us. "Head of the House, huh? How do you even know this is the same monkey?"

How many golden lion tamarin monkeys did he expect to be running around in Eleanor Tinsley Park? "Rosebud, sing."

The monkey raised her adorable head, opened her mouth, and trilled like a little bird.

The three MII employees stared at her. Here's hoping for logic and reason...

"This proves nothing," the woman announced.

As it happened so often with our species, logical reasoning was discarded in favor of the overpowering need to be right, facts and consequences be damned.

"What about now?" Leon asked. "Can I kill one? Just one."

Leon was extremely selective about shooting people, but the MII agents drew on me and Cornelius, and his protective instinct kicked into the overdrive. If they raised their guns another two inches, they would die, and my cousin was doing his best deranged rattlesnake act to keep that from happening.

Leon wagged his eyebrows at me.

"No," I told him.

"I said please. What about the kneecaps? I can shoot them in the kneecaps, and they won't die. They won't be happy, but they won't die."

"No." I turned to Cornelius. "Is there any way to retrieve her without hurting them?"

He smiled and looked to the sky.

Cornelius Maddox Harrison didn't look particularly threatening. He was white and thirty-one years old, of average build and below average height. His dark blond hair was trimmed by a professional stylist into a short but flattering cut. His features were attractive, his jaw clean shaven, and his blue eyes were always quiet, calm, and just a little distant. The three MII agents took one look at his face and his badass ensemble of light khaki pants and a white dress shirt with the sleeves rolled up to his elbows and decided they had nothing to worry about. Next to him, dark haired, tan, and lean Leon radiated menace and kept making threats, so they judged him to be the bigger risk.

"This has been fun and all," the older MII agent said. "But playtime is over, and we have an actual job to do."

A reddish-brown hawk plummeted from the sky, plucked the monkey from the pole, swooped over the agents, and dropped Rosebud into Cornelius' hand. The monkey scampered up Cornelius' arm and onto his shoulder, hugged his neck, and trilled into his ear. The chicken hawk flew to our left and perched on the limb of a red myrtle growing by the sidewalk.

"Well, shit," the woman said.

"Feel free to report this to Augustine," I told them. "He has my number."

And if he had a problem with it, I would smooth it over. Augustine Montgomery and our family had a complicated relationship. I'd studied him with the same dedication I used to study complex equations, so if he ever became a threat, I could neutralize him.

The older of the men gave us a hard stare. His firearm crept up an inch. "Where do you think you're going?"

I snapped my Prime face on. "Leon, if he targets us, cripple him."

Leon's lips stretched into a soft dreamy smile.

People in the violence business quickly learned to recognize other professionals. The MII agents were well trained and experienced, because Augustine prided himself on quality. They looked into my cousin's eyes and they knew that Leon was all in. There was no fear or apprehension there. He enjoyed what he did, and given permission, he wouldn't hesitate.

Then they looked at me. Over the past six months I'd become adept at assuming my Head of the House persona. It came naturally now, without any strain, and it saved bullets and heartache. My eyes told them that I didn't care about their lives or their survival. If they made themselves into an obstacle, I would have them removed. It didn't matter what I wore, how old I was, or what words I said. That look would tell them everything they needed to know.

The tense silence stretched.

The woman whipped out her cell phone and turned away, dialing a number. The two men lowered their guns.

Oh good. Everyone would get to go home.

Augustine's people marched toward the river, the shorter man in the lead, and turned right, aiming for the small parking lot where I had parked Hammer, the custom armored SUV Grandma Frida made for me. They gave us a wide berth. We watched them go. No reason to force another confrontation in the parking lot.

We'd been looking for Rosebud for the last week, ever since Cornelius took the case. Her owner, a twelve-year-old girl, was so traumatized by the theft, she had to be sedated. Finding the little monkey trumped the rest of our case load. We accepted this job pro bono, because snatching a service animal from a child in a wheelchair was a heinous act and someone had to make it right.

Scouring Houston in 100-degree heat looking for a monkey the size of a large squirrel took a lot of effort. I barely managed five hours of sleep in the last forty-eight, but every bit of my sweat would be worth it if I could see Maya hug her monkey.

Cornelius smiled again. "I do so love happy endings."

"Happy ending for you, maybe," Leon grumbled. "I didn't get to shoot anybody."

First, we would deliver Rosebud to Maya, and then I would go home, and take a shower, and then a long happy nap...

Cornelius shook his head. "Your reliance on violence is quite disturbing. What happens when you meet someone faster than you?"

My cousin pondered it. "I'll be dead, and it won't matter?"

Talon took to the air with a shriek, swooping over Buffalo Bayou River. Leon and Cornelius stopped at the same time. Cornelius frowned, looking at the murky waters to the left of a large tree.

Directly in front of us, a narrow strip of mowed lawn hugged the sidewalk. Past the grass, the ground sloped sharply, hidden by

125

tall weeds all the way to the river that stretched to Memorial Parkway Bridge in the distance.

The river lay placid. Not even a ripple troubled the surface.

I glanced at Leon. A second ago his hands were empty. Now he held a Sig P226 in one hand and a Glock 17 in the other. It gave him thirty-two rounds of 9mm ammunition. He only needed one round to make a kill.

"What is it?" I asked quietly.

"I don't know," Leon said.

"The hawk is scared," Cornelius said.

The surface of the river was still and shining slightly, reflecting the sunlight like a tarnished dime.

The distance in Cornelius' eyes grew deeper. "Something's coming," he whispered.

We had no reason to hang around and wait for it. "Let's go."

I turned right and sped up toward our vehicles. Leon and Cornelius followed.

Ahead the shorter of the MII agents was almost to the lot. The woman trailed him, while the taller agent brought up the rear.

A green body burst through the weeds. Eight feet long and four feet tall, it scrambled forward on two big muscular legs, dragging the long scaly tail fringed with bright carmine fins. A blood-red crested fin with foot-long spikes thrust from its spine. Its head could have belonged to an aquatic dinosaur or a prehistoric crocodile -- huge pincher-like jaws that opened like giant scissors studded with conical fangs designed to grab and hold struggling prey while the beast pulled them under. Two pairs of small eyes, sunken deep into its skull, glowed with violet.

This didn't look like anything our planet had birthed. It was either some magic experiment gone haywire or a summon from arcane realm.

We would need bigger guns.

The beast rushed across the grass. The taller MII agent was directly in its path.

"Run!" Leon and I screamed at the same time.

The man whipped around. For a frantic half-second he froze, then jerked his gun up, and fired at the creature. Bullets bit into the beast and glanced off its thick scales.

The two other MII agents pivoted to the creature and opened fire. I sprinted to Hammer and the combat shotgun inside it. Leon dashed after me, trying to get a better angle on the creature. Cornelius followed.

Augustine's people emptied their magazines into the beast. It plowed through them, knocking them aside, shockingly fast. Purple blood stained its sides, but the wounds barely bled, as if the bullets had merely chipped its scales.

The beast's gaze locked on me. It ignored the agents and hauled itself toward me, the two massive paws gouging the turf with red claws.

Leon fired a two-bullet burst from each gun. Four bloody holes gaped where the creature's beady eyes used to be. It roared, stumbled, and crashed to the ground.

I halted. Cornelius ran past me to the lot.

The female MII agent rose slowly. Her tall friend stared at a bright red gash in his bare thigh. His left pant leg hung in bloody shreds around his ankle. He shifted his weight. Blood poured from the wound and I saw a glimpse of bone inside. The agent gaped at it, wide-eyed, clearly in shock.

"Holy shit," the shorter MII agent muttered and snapped a new magazine into his HK45.

At the edge of the parking lot, Cornelius spun around and waved his arms toward the river. "Don't stop! There's more! More are coming!"

Green beasts poured through the weeds, a mass of scaled

bodies, finned tails, and fanged jaws, and in its center, buried under the creatures, a dense knot of magic pulsated like an invisible beacon. The knot's magic splayed out, touched me, and broke around my power, like a wave against a breaker. A sea of violet eyes focused on me.

The pack charged.

Whatever it was emanating magic in the center of the pack controlled them. If I had a second, I could've fought it with my magic, but the cluster of bodies was too thick, and the beasts came too fast.

I turned and sprinted to Hammer. The thing's magic followed me, pinging from my mind like radar. I didn't need to look back to know the pack had turned to chase me.

Ahead Cornelius jerked a car remote from his pocket. The lights of his BMW hybrid flashed. The hatchback rose and a massive blue beast tore out, a tiger on steroids, with glossy indigo fur splattered with black and pale blue rosettes.

Zeus landed, roared, flashing fangs the size of steak knives, and bounded across the parking lot. The fringe of tentacles around his neck unfurled, individual tendrils writhing. We passed each other, him sprinting at the creatures and me running in the opposite direction for the Hammer.

Gunfire popped behind me like firecrackers going off – Leon, thinning the pack. He'd run out of bullets before they ran out of bodies.

I jumped into Hammer, mashed the brake, and pushed the ignition switch. The engine roared. Cornelius flung the passenger door open and landed in the seat. I stepped on it. Hammer's custom engine kicked into gear. We shot forward and jumped the curb onto the grass.

In front of us the lawn churned with bodies. A trail of scaled corpses stretched to the left, piling up at the curb of Allen Parkway. Across the street, Leon methodically sank bullets into the creatures in short bursts, using traffic as cover. Zeus snarled next to him. A scaled beast lay nearby and Zeus raked it with his claws to underscore his point.

On our right the female agent and the leader had put their arms under the injured man's shoulders and staggered toward the parking lot. He hung limp, dragging his bleeding leg behind him. The leading beasts on the left snapped their jaws only feet behind them.

No people would be mauled by these things today if I could help it.

I steered right, cutting the creatures off from the MII agents at a sharp angle. The enormously heavy bulk of Hammer smashed into the closest creature with a wet crunch. Hammer careened as we rolled over a body. We burst through the edge of the pack into the clear. I put my foot down on the accelerator, tearing down the lawn. Behind me the pack thinned out, as the creatures got into each other's way trying to turn to follow us. For a moment, the cluster of bodies dispersed. Something spun in their center, something metal, round and glowing. The strange magic knot.

"You see it?"

"I see it." Cornelius pulled the tactical shotgun from the floor-boards and pumped it.

"Can you reach their minds?"

"No. They're too preoccupied."

Asking him what that meant now would distract him. I made a hard left, clipping what was once the back of the pack, knocking the stragglers out of the way.

"Ready," Cornelius said, his voice calm.

I hit the button to lower the front windows and cut straight through the pack, mowing a diagonal line to the left. The churning rolling thing spun on our right, drawing tight circles on the grass. Cornelius stuck the barrel of the shotgun out the window and fired.

BOOM.

My ears rang.

BOOM.

"One more time," Cornelius said, as if asking for another cup of tea.

We flashed by the pack, smashed head on into a beast, and I veered right and jumped the curb back into the parking lot. The MII vehicle, a silver Jeep Grand Cherokee, peeled out onto the Allen Parkway with a squeal of tires. The stench of burning rubber blew into the cabin.

"You're welcome." Cornelius reloaded.

I made a hard right onto the parkway. The pack of beasts streaked by on our right.

BOOM.

BOOM.

"Didn't get it," Cornelius said. "The slugs bounced off. There's something alive inside it."

"Animal?"

"Not exactly."

If it was alive, we could kill it.

We could drive around until the pack tired enough to slow down, grab Leon and Zeus, and drive off, but then these things would rampage through Houston. There was a group of kids playing just a quarter of a mile down the road. We had passed them and the adults who were watching them on our way in to retrieve Rosebud.

Rosebud!

"Where is the monkey?"

"Safe in the BMW."

Oh good. Good, good, good.

I pulled a sharp U turn and sped down the street back toward the parking lot. The beasts scrambled to follow. The gaps between the bodies widened to several feet and I saw the source of magic. Two metals rings, spinning one inside the other, like a gyroscope. A small blue glow hovered between them.

We passed Leon. He pointed to the glowing thing with his Sig and pretended to smash the two guns in his hands together. *Ram it.* Thank you, Captain Strategy, I got it. That thing had survived the river. If I hit it with Hammer, it might just bounce aside, and if it was arcane, there was no telling what sort of damage it would do to the car.

The gyroscope spun too fast for Cornelius' rounds to penetrate. We had to destroy it. This would require precision.

"Rapier?" I asked.

"One moment." Cornelius turned and hit the switch on the console between our seats. Most SUV vehicles had two front seats and a wide back seat designed to seat three. Hammer had four seats with a long, custom-built console storage running lengthwise between them. The console popped open, and a weapon shelf sprang up, offering a choice of two blades and two guns secured by prongs.

I pulled another U turn. A white truck screeched to a stop in front of me. The driver laid on the horn, saw the beasts, and reversed down the street at breakneck speed.

"Got it." Cornelius turned back in his seat, my rapier in his hand.

I aimed Hammer at the gyroscope. Bodies slammed against the car.

"This is foolhardy," Cornelius advised. "What if it explodes?"

"Then I'll be dead, and I won't care," I quoted.

"Using Leon as inspiration is a doubtful survival strategy."

I slammed on the brakes. Hammer slid across the lawn and

stopped. I jumped out of the SUV. The rotating thing spun only fifty feet away from me. I sprinted to it.

A beast lunged at me. I jumped aside and kept running.

Behind me Hammer thundered, as Cornelius revved the engine to distract them.

The air turned to fire in my lungs. I dodged a beast, another…

Thirty feet.

The shining object pinged me with its magic.

Twenty.

Ten.

The metal rings spun in front of me, two feet wide, splattered with slime and algae. Inside a flower bud glowed, a brilliant electric blue lotus woven of pure magic and just about to bloom.

My family's magic coursed through me, guiding my thrust. I stabbed it.

The bud burst, sending a cloud of luminescent sparks into the air. The blue glow vanished. The rings stopped spinning. The beasts around me froze.

For a torturous moment nothing moved.

The creatures stared at me. I stared back.

The pack turned and made a break for the river.

It was over.

The relief washed over me. A steady rhythmic noise came into focus, and I realized it was my heart racing in my chest. My knees shook. A bitter metallic patina coated my tongue. My body couldn't figure out if it was hot or cold. The world felt wrong, as if I had been poisoned.

The ruins of the device lay in front of me. I tried to take a step. My leg folded under me, the ground decided to spontaneously tilt to the side, and I almost wiped out on a perfectly level lawn. Too much adrenaline. Nothing to do but wait it out. Some people were born for the knife's edge intensity of combat. I wasn't one of them.

Focusing on something to distract myself usually helped. I crouched and scrutinized the rings. The metal didn't look exactly like steel, but it might have been some sort of iron alloy. A string of glyphs ran the circumference of each ring.

I pulled my phone out of my pocket and snapped a pic.

The rings fit inside each other, the largest about three inches smaller than the larger one. The flower stalk was attached to the bottom of the inner ring. No, not attached. It grew from the inner ring, seamlessly protruding from the metal.

How?

I picked up the ring and tugged on the stalk. It held. I ran my fingers along the flower. Toward the severed end, where the flower bud had been, the texture felt like a typical plant. But the lower I moved my fingers, the more metallic the texture became. A true biomechanical meld. To my knowledge, no mage had yet achieved it.

Hammer rolled up next to me. Cornelius jumped out. Pale purple blood splattered the armored vehicle's custom grille guard. Bits and pieces of alien flesh hung from the metal.

"Are you alright?" Cornelius asked.

No. "Yes. I'm so sorry," I told him. "I know this was very unpleasant for you."

Animal mages formed a special bond with a few chosen animals, but they cared about all of them, and we had just mowed down at least a dozen, maybe more.

Cornelius nodded. "Thank you for your concern. They weren't true animals in the native sense of the world. It helped some."

"Is this a summon?" I asked.

Cornelius shook his head. "I don't think so. They feel slightly similar to Zeus. Not of Earth but not completely of the arcane realm either."

"Earlier you said they were too 'preoccupied' to reach?"

Cornelius frowned and nodded at the rings and the bud within. "This object emitted magic."

"I felt it."

"The emissions were so dense, they effectively deafened the creatures. They couldn't feel me. I'd tried to contact the object itself, but the biological component of it is so primitive, it was like trying to communicate with a sea sponge."

The House lab scenario looked more and more likely. If these proto-crocodiles had come out of the arcane realm, we would have seen a summoner and a portal. Massive holes in reality were kind of hard to miss.

Linus would just love this.

Speaking of Linus… I pulled out my phone and dialed his number. One beep, two, three…

At the other end of the lawn Leon jogged across the road, Zeus in tow.

The phone kept ringing. Officially Linus Duncan was retired. In reality, he still served the state of Texas in a new, more frightening capacity, and I was his deputy. He always answered my calls.

Beep. Another.

Linus' voice came on the line. "Yes?"

"I was attacked by magic monsters in Eleanor Tinsley Park. They were controlled by a biomechanical device powered with magic."

Leon ran up and halted next to me.

"Do you require assistance?" Linus asked.

"Not anymore."

"Show me."

I activated facetime, switched the camera, and panned the

phone, capturing the device, the corpses, and the fleeing creatures. On the screen, Linus stared into the phone. In his sixties, still fit, with thick salt and pepper hair, Linus always had the Texas tan. His features were handsome and bold, a square jaw framed by a short beard, prominent nose, thick dark eyebrows, and dark eyes. He smiled easily and when he paid attention to you, you felt special. If you asked ten people who just met him to describe him, they would all say one word – charming.

The man looking back at me from the phone was the real Linus Duncan, a Prime, former Speaker of the Texas Assembly, focused, sharp, his dark eyes merciless. He looked like an old tiger who spotted an intruder in his domain and was sharpening his claws for the kill. A dry staccato came through the phone, a rhythmic thud-thud-thud, followed by a mechanical whine. Linus' turrets. He was under attack.

Who in the world would assault Linus Duncan in his home? He was a Hephaestus mage. He made lethal firearms out of discarded paperclips and duct tape and his house packed enough firepower to wipe out an elite battalion in minutes.

They attacked me and Linus simultaneously. The thought burned a trail through my mind like a comet.

"Disengage," Linus said. "Go straight to MII, take over the Morton case, use the badge. Repeat."

"Go straight to MII, show the badge, take over the Morton case."

Usually Linus brought me in after the jurisdiction had been established. In the last six months, I've had to use my badge exactly once, to take over an FBI investigation. To say they had been unhappy about it would be a gross understatement.

"I'll send the files." Linus hung up.

"What are we doing?" My cousin asked.

"You're driving me to MII."

"I'll follow." Cornelius sprinted to the parking lot, Zeus on his heels, bounding like an overly enthusiastic kitten.

I grabbed the device. The metal rings were slick with mud and slime. I walked to Hammer, threw the device into the bin in the back, and jumped into the passenger seat.

In the distance, police sirens wailed, getting closer.

———

Preorder EMERALD BLAZE on your retailer of choice here!

ALSO BY ILONA ANDREWS

Kate Daniels Series

MAGIC BITES

MAGIC BLEEDS

MAGIC BURNS

MAGIC STRIKES

MAGIC MOURNS

MAGIC BLEEDS

MAGIC DREAMS

MAGIC SLAYS

GUNMETAL MAGIC

MAGIC GIFTS

MAGIC RISES

MAGIC BREAKS

MAGIC STEALS

MAGIC SHIFTS

MAGIC STARS

MAGIC BINDS

MAGIC TRIUMPHS

The Iron Covenant

IRON AND MAGIC

UNTITLED IRON AND MAGIC #2

Hidden Legacy Series

BURN FOR ME

WHITE HOT

WILDFIRE

DIAMOND FIRE

SAPPHIRE FLAMES

EMERALD BLAZE

Innkeeper Chronicles Series

CLEAN SWEEP

SWEEP IN PEACE

ONE FELL SWEEP

SWEEP OF THE BLADE

The Edge Series

ON THE EDGE

BAYOU MOON

FATE'S EDGE

STEEL'S EDGE

CPSIA information can be obtained
at www.ICGtesting.com
Printed in the USA
BVHW040815260122
627252BV00013B/222